Forging North

Life on the Alaska Frontier

G.E. Sherman

Copyright ©2012 G.E. Sherman

ISBN-13: 978-1477559161
ISBN-10: 1477559167

This work is historical fiction. Some of the incidents described herein may not exactly align with actual events of
the period. All the characters in this book are fictional.

To Stella Mae

Books in the
Life on the Alaska Frontier series

1. FORGING NORTH

2. FORTYMILE

3. HEARTBREAK CABIN

"Life is not always a matter of holding good cards, but sometimes, playing a poor hand well."
  Jack London

Chapter 1

Thomas Everton Thornton leaned against the rail and took a long drag on his cigarette, listening to the groans and creaks of the old ship as it wrestled with the swells. The April sun was setting, back lighting the rugged mountain peaks of Southcentral Alaska as the *S.S. North Wind* steamed steadily past, the drumming of her engines lulling Thomas into a state of drowsiness.

He was thankful the trip on the tired steamer had so far been uneventful, sailing from Seattle through the Inside Passage and across the Gulf of Alaska. On schedule and making good time, the *North Wind* was scheduled to make landing in Valdez in about two days time. He was anxious, dreaming of all that was before him once he arrived.

"Well what do you think of this part of the world son?"

The question startled Thomas who was still daydreaming. Turning from the rail he saw Samuel Pierce, smiling from under his battered seaman's cap. They had met when boarding in Seattle, but Thomas hadn't seen him in the three days since they set sail.

"It's very big," said Thomas. "I was thinking of how long it is going to take."

"How long what's going to take?"

"How long it will take me to get to the gold fields."

"You newcomers are all alike; in a big hurry to strike it rich. This is my third trip and I'm still looking for the pot of gold."

"Really? How long have you been prospecting in Alaska?"

"I came to the Interior in '86, right after the strike on the Fortymile. Got there too late; all the good ground was claimed and spent the whole summer digging worthless dirt. Then they struck on the Klondike in '96 so I gave it another try but had lot's of trouble."

"What kind of trouble?"

"Lost all my supplies on the Yukon when my boat capsized. Barely made it to shore and spent days waiting for help."

Thomas knew nearly everything about the rush to the Klondike. He had read every article in the Seattle paper and hung on every word any time it was mentioned. If he wasn't nearly broke at the time, he would have been on the first steamer north.

"Sounds like you've had a lot of misfortune," said Thomas. "Where are you headed now?"

"Well, after two years of scratching around

for a grubstake I'm going to head down the Yukon River again and see if I can't find some virgin ground," said Pierce, looking away from Thomas as he spoke.

Thomas sensed a change in Pierce's demeanor, but he couldn't put his finger on it. "I hope you have better luck this time."

"As do I," said Pierce. "Where you headed once we get to Valdez?"

"Well, I really would like to get into the Interior, I hear there is still some virgin ground left if I can get there in time."

"Maybe. Don't get too impatient young man. You can't get in too much of a hurry in this country. When you get in a hurry you get careless, and when you get careless in Alaska, she'll kill you."

Thomas looked out across the swells at the snow-dusted mountains barely visible in the twilight. He was so far from his roots; that little farm in the Midwest where he had grown up. He always thought of himself as an adventurer, though nothing in his twenty-five years would lead one to think so. Now he was far out of his element.

He took another drag on his cigarette and said, "I'm well aware of the dangers," knowing full well he was fooling himself.

"Well the Interior is a big place, lot's of opportunity for trouble," said Pierce dryly. "How much do you know about mining?"

"Well, not much really. I've never really used a gold pan," said Thomas, immediately regretting the statement.

Pierce laughed. "So you don't know how to use a gold pan. Do you know what a sluice box is?"

"Sure. I've seen a picture or two, and a fellow I worked with on the docks told me all about them."

"Can you build one?"

Thomas could see where this was going. "Well I don't know how but I'm sure I can figure it out."

"Never used a gold pan, don't know what a sluice box looks like. I hope you can at least run a number two shovel."

"I know more than you think," said Thomas, sighing as he flicked his cigarette into the swells below.

"Doesn't sound like it to me son. I suppose you've got all your supplies and equipment with you?"

"No, I plan to buy everything I need when I

get to Alaska."

"Hmm...how about money then? Things cost way more in Alaska than they do in Seattle. How much money you got with you?" said Pierce, leaning in close to Thomas.

"I've got enough to last me at least a year, tucked away right here," said Thomas, patting his vest pocket. "I worked long and hard on the Seattle docks to save it up."

"Well at least that's something," said Pierce, stepping back. "If I can be of help to you son, let me know. Maybe we'll meet out there somewhere, and you can buy me a drink after you strike it rich," he said as he walked away.

Thomas didn't care much for how the conversation had turned. Pierce had placed even more doubt in his mind. *Maybe I don't have enough money,* he thought.

He had tried to be frugal; passage on the *North Wind* had cost him little. She was the cheapest thing headed north at the time, though she lacked the refinement of the steamers in the Alaska Steamship Company's fleet, badly needed paint, and as far as Thomas could tell, continually strained to stay together with each passing swell.

He pulled his tobacco pouch from his vest

pocket and paused. Emily had begged him not to go, well aware of the dangers and evil of the gold rush camps. *I wonder how much I hurt her by leaving*, he thought, the image of those sad blue eyes, the tears running down her cheek burned an indelible image in his mind. His empty words promising a safe return had done little to comfort her. *Was this any way to treat a girl who was the single greatest thing that has ever happened to me?*, he thought, the guilt welling up within him. But he couldn't dwell on that now.

As Thomas lit his cigarette he thought about Old Man Haskel. He was the one who had planted the seeds for this adventure years ago, with his tales of gold nuggets for the taking and the easy money to be had by those just brave enough to venture north. Thomas recalled how he first met him on the docks where they worked together loading and unloading cargo steamers. Haskel had a nearly two ounce gold nugget on a chain he wore around his neck. Thomas saw it everyday they worked together and became entranced by the appeal of its luster. Holding that nugget in his hand sparked something in him; he wasn't sure if it was wanderlust or greed, but he liked it.

Haskel had given up the gold fields, having lost most of his money through poor investments and riotous living. The nugget was his one treasure and the only evidence of his former life. He had abandoned the dream and returned to steady work, but that didn't quell his passion for telling stories of gold and the quest for it.

Something about those tales struck a chord with Thomas. The whole idea, the adventure, the riches, appealed to him, despite the fact the majority of gold seekers from previous stampedes had gone home broke or discouraged. A good number of them died trying. Of course, Thomas tried not to think about that too much. Gold fever had a tendency to make one forget the harsh realities.

Three days ago he was certain he could succeed where others failed; now he wasn't so sure.

The chill of the night air turned him from the rail and he headed for his berth. He was in over his head and he knew it.

* * *

The *North Wind* eased slowly into the dock, deck hands rushing about to cast lines ashore. Almost immediately after docking, before Thomas had a chance to get near the gang plank, the so-called experts rushed on board with promises of easy fortunes and lots of help, all for a price of course. For several minutes there was utter chaos while the deck hands attempted to clear the way to the gang plank.

Thomas had never seen anything like it in his whole life. People pushing and shoving to get on and off the ship, nearly knocking each other over. Thomas moved towards the gang blank too early and was rammed from behind, knocking him into the railing and nearly causing his bag to go overboard.

"Watch it," Thomas said sternly as he turned and faced the offender.

"Sorry," said the scrawny man with a pointy beard as he used his elbow to navigate around Thomas.

Unbelievable, thought Thomas. He was as anxious as anyone to exit the ship, but not at the expense of civility. He stepped back out of the way and decided to wait, looking to shore in anticipation. Pierce had somehow made it off the ship and was walking down the muddy path that served as a street, his bag in one hand and a bottle in the other. Thomas briefly thought about calling out to him but knew he would never be heard over the sea of voices currently occupying the ship.

Slowly the crowd thinned and Thomas was able to make his way down the gang plank and along the boardwalk, finally setting foot on Alaska soil. For a moment, he took in a deep breath and marveled at the sights and sounds around him. The din of the crowd grew distant as he took in the majesty of the snow capped mountains and glaciers that surrounded him. Amid that muddy outwash plain of the Valdez Glacier, even the air smelled different, electrifying. He was finally here and he savored the moment. It was over too soon; the noise on the dock grabbed his attention.

The confused mass of passengers was shoving its way to the cargo area to claim equipment. Shouting and cursing ensued as men argued over who was first in line. Others hollered at the cargo agent to make sure he didn't give away their belongings to the wrong person. All in all it was quite a sight. Fortunately for Thomas he was able to avoid the fray, having just a pack sack and large bag which he had kept with him on board.

Thomas elbowed his way through the surging crowd and headed up the muddy street, looking for a place to bunk. He had brought minimal supplies with him and was still in need of food and sound advice. Having been forewarned by many, Thomas knew to be on the lookout for those who would gladly relieve him of his money. He had been fortunate to be one of the last to leave the ship; most of the hawkers had already found victims or had gone back to their hovels.

First order of business was a place to stay. Having made no firm plans about what he would do once he arrived, Thomas now found himself somewhat out of sorts. As he passed the baggage area he came upon a number of wagons and drivers, waiting for a fare.

"Excuse me," he said to the closest driver. "Can you tell me where I can find a place to stay for the night?"

The driver looked at him and laughed, "Going to be tough, there's over three hundred people passing through here every day."

"Surely there must be some place to stay."

"Well, if you can beat the crowd you might get lucky but I hope you brought a tent with you," said the driver, laughing again. "You need a ride?"

"No, I'll walk," said Thomas. "Just point me in the right direction."

The driver looked perturbed at losing a fare, but pointed Thomas towards the nearest side street. "Just head up to the end of that street and hang a left, then go down aways until you get to the alley on the right. You'll find the hotel on the cross street at the end of the alley."

"How far is it?" asked Thomas.

"Not very far; you sure you don't want to ride?"

Thomas declined and thanked the driver, who responded with a sneer and turned away.

There was still a lot of commotion in the streets; wagons hauling freight this way and that, men tramping through the ankle deep mud with packs; picks and shovels poking out in all directions.

As he walked up the street away from the dock and into the alley, noise faded and the late afternoon shadows fell around him. Rough lumber shanties lined the alley, shading the final moments of warmth as the sun set. Thomas quickened his pace to beat the impending darkness, worried he would be spending the night on the street.

"You There!" a deep voice cried out from behind him. *Who would be...* the thought formed as he started to turn. In mid-turn a shot rang out. Thomas felt a strange sensation in his shoulder as the impact spun him to the right. Before the sensation changed to searing pain, he collapsed face first into the mud.

Chapter 2

The shadowy figure rifled through Thomas' belongings as he lay in the mud. The evening shadows were upon them and cloaked the thief's movements. *Money, a pocket watch, clothes-good; letters-leave them.* He worked quickly, stripping Thomas of anything of value. Thomas moaned as consciousness tried to return. The thief finished going through the pack, bag, and wallet and, looking around to see if he had been discovered, slogged off into the night.

Thomas woke with a start. His shoulder was stiff and he realized he was lying in the muddy street. He didn't know how long he had been out, but knew something was very wrong and he had to get up. He raised up and the searing pain struck him like a hammer. The blackness returned as consciousness left him and he sank back into the cold, dank mud.

* * *

"Now lie still or you'll start bleeding again" a distant voice said. The fog in his head began to clear and slowly the surroundings came into view. To his surprise, the sun was glistening through a window, a gentle breeze blowing across the room. A table, chairs, and a figure slowly came into view.

"Where am I?"

"You are in my boarding house," said the woman as she checked his wound for signs of bleeding.

The pain in his shoulder grabbed his attention, sparking the vague memory of lying in the cold mud.

"What happened to me?"

"About all I know is a couple of the boys found you in the side street, shot through the shoulder and bleeding. They picked you up and brought you to me since I'm about the closest thing there is to a doctor around here." she said. "Lucky those boys came across you, most would have left you lie."

"Who are you?" said Thomas as he tried to sit up.

"My name is Stella Mae and I've been taking care of you—now lie still or you're going to start bleeding all over my clean sheets."

"How bad is it?" asked Thomas.

"You were lucky, your wound was enough to put you down but missed your vitals. Just passed through the upper shoulder and must have missed your lungs or you wouldn't be here now.

I think you're going to be all right, but you won't be swinging a pick for a while."

Thomas slumped back onto the bed, a great wave of fatigue coming over him as though he could sleep forever. This wasn't in his plans; derailed before he even got started.

"How long have I been here?" he asked, suppressing the pain in his voice.

"Three days. You were in pretty bad shape when they brought you in. You didn't make it far from the boat. I don't know what things are coming to," she said with a tone of disappointment in her voice. "Used to be people here were friendly and helpful, but I'm afraid the greed and lust for gold has brought us many who would kill for a mere dollar."

"I feel so tired," said Thomas.

"Well, it's going to take a while for you to recover. You lost a fair amount of blood."

Suddenly panic swept over him. "Where are my things?" he said, looking frantically around the room.

Stella placed her hand on his arm and said, "Well son, there wasn't much left. Whoever shot you took most anything of value. About the only thing you have left is an empty pack."

Thomas laid his head back and closed his

eyes as a whole range of emotions—anger, despair, and frustration swept over him. He couldn't believe his situation, stranded in a strange place, hurt, and with nothing to his name. *Well Pappy, I guess you were right*, Thomas thought. *I guess I am a fool for leaving the farm...*

Opening his eyes, Thomas looked at the woman he was now dependent upon. She was the motherly looking type, probably in her early fifties. She had graying hair and a pleasant look about her. Thomas wondered what it took for a woman to live on the frontier, wondered how Emily would fare in such a place.

"Whoever robbed you did leave you one thing; the letters," said Stella.

"Letters?"

"You know—the letters from Emily. I hope you don't mind, but I read them to see if you had family somewhere that should know what happened to you, especially if you didn't pull through."

"Oh, yes, guess I'm still a bit foggy," said Thomas.

He had kept every letter Emily wrote him while he was back in Iowa last year, settling the affairs of his father who had died unexpectedly. After the funeral, Thomas spent several

months putting things in order, including bringing in the crop of corn. His mother pleaded
with him to stay and work the farm but he had
other plans, finally persuading her to sell and
move to the city. He wished he could see her
now.

"You rest now," Stella said as she opened the
door and paused. "Oh, by the way, I sent word
to Emily," she said as she closed the door.

Chapter 3

Emily Palmer sat on the edge of the bay window seat, looking across the garden to the lake, wondering where Thomas was this very moment. She gazed at the boats sailing on the water, the gentle afternoon breeze moving them lazily along. Father and Mother had gone to yet another of their social gatherings, leaving Emily to stare out the window at the shimmering shapes dancing on the lake.

She was a little over five feet tall, with light brown hair, a petite figure, and piercing blue eyes. She had many suitors, most sons of important society people whose fathers were doctors, lawyers, or politicians. None had captured her fancy and each relationship was merely social—until she met Thomas.

She thought about how they had met, how she had been attracted to his gentleness surrounded by those rough edges. He was tall and handsome, and she loved how his curly brown hair tickled his collar. Her mother had been against her seeing him at first; she being from a family of means and him just a farmer turned starry-eyed dreamer. All the talk of gold and riches in Alaska hadn't helped any either. Yet slowly her parents had grown to appreciate Thomas' sincerity and the fact he truly cared for her.

Mulling it over in her mind, Emily thought perhaps Father secretly desired the adventure Thomas spoke of so vividly. Before Thomas left, Father had spent many hours in the den with him, listening to his plans and offering advice and counsel. That was two months ago and now he was gone, even though she had pleaded with him not to go. Thomas had said Alaska was no place for her; that he would return in a season and then they would be married, once he found his fortune.

Emily knew the stories of great wealth, but she could also read. The newspaper repeatedly told of those who had lost all, some including their lives, in the search for gold far from home. It was too much for her to think about, and yet she couldn't put it out of her mind. *Thomas, Thomas...*

Looking away from the window she hung her head as the tears began to flow again.

"Emily" John Palmer called as he and Mrs. Palmer entered the front door.

"Emily, we have word from Alaska!"

* * *

At the sound of her father's voice, Emily rushed from the room and down the stairs, her heart flooded with excitement, yet mixed with fear and dread. She didn't realize Thomas would send word so soon.

Her father and mother met her at the bottom of the stairs. Mr. Palmer was holding an envelope addressed to Emily.

"I'm sure it's good news dear," her mother said, trying to assuage Emily's concerns.

With shaking hands, Emily took the envelope from her father and slowly opened it.

"It's not from Thomas!"

```
May 13, 1903

To: Miss Emily Palmer:

Dear Miss Emily,

My name is Stella Mae Baird.  Your
young gentleman friend Thomas was
injured in an unfortunate encounter
three days ago.  I found your name and
address in the letters he was
carrying.  He is in my care and at
present has not regained
consciousness.  I believe he will
recover if I can keep his wound from
becoming infected.  The bullet missed
his lungs and heart.  Please pass word
on to his family, if he has any.

Sincerely,

Stella Mae Baird
```

Emily's hands dropped to her side and her face went blank.

"What is it Emily? What does it say?" her father asked.

Emily slowly handed him the letter and sank to the stairs, her face in her hands. John Palmer read the letter aloud, pausing as he came to the part about the bullet. Emily was sobbing, her mother at her side trying to comfort her, but meeting with little success.

It had taken three weeks for the letter to reach them. It would be six more weeks before they could receive word about Thomas, even if they sent an inquiry today.

"I'm sure he is fine, Emily. He's young and strong and sounds like he is in good hands" her father said. He had no reason to be optimistic, but was trying to comfort Emily with his reasoning.

"Yes, dear, I'm sure he's fine," her mother added.

Emily looked up, tears streaking her face. "We must go to him," she said with determination in her voice.

Mrs. Palmer shot a glance at her husband. *Now what shall we do...* she thought.

"Emily, why don't you go back upstairs and get some rest, we can talk about this in the morning," said John.

"I can't sleep, I'm too worried about Thomas," she said, wiping the tears with the back of her hand.

"I know you're worried, but staying up and fretting about it won't help in the least."

"I want to go to him. I have to know."

"Go on now, up to your room and we will sort this out tomorrow; I promise," said her father.

Emily reluctantly obeyed and slowly climbed the stairs, weeping the whole way. Hearing her door close, John and Lydia Palmer retired to the sitting room.

"She can't be serious about going to find that boy," Lydia said adamantly.

"Six weeks is a long time to wait for word," said John.

"But word may already be on the way. It would be foolish to consider a trip to Alaska when we don't even know for sure what has happened to him." Lydia had definite feelings about this and wasn't about to let a nineteen year old girl trounce off to a place like the mining camps of Alaska.

"Don't you agree?" she asked her husband.

"I agree word may be on the way, and yet I sympathize with Emily's need to know as soon as possible."

"Surely you are not suggesting she should go!" Lydia said in disbelief.

"No, I'm not. I shall go with her." said John, his gaze fixed out the window at the lake.

"I won't have it. This is preposterous! The boy is probably fine and we will hear from him any day," Lydia said as she jumped to her feet. "I knew you still harbored some dream of being a pioneer or whatever you call it. That boy has put fool ideas in your head and you should be old enough to realize it."

Lydia had always been a loving wife, and many people considered her somewhat reserved. But there was a side to her most people had never seen. It had surfaced and she held none of her feelings back.

"Perhaps you are right," John said. "Or perhaps we should all go," he said, a faint smile appearing on his lips.

"Surely you aren't willing to throw all we have away—to risk our family. We have all we need here. There is no need for us to go off on a wild chase in search of gold."

"I never said anything about searching for gold. We are talking of finding Thomas for Emily's sake."

"I still think we should send word. Can't we send a telegram?"

"I don't know if there is telegraph service to Valdez, although we may be able to send a message to some place in Alaska and have it delivered. That may be quicker."

Yet he had his doubts. He had no idea of conditions in Alaska. The fact it took three weeks by boat to get the message from Alaska made John realize how far away Thomas really was.

"Let's not discuss this any further," Lydia said. "Tomorrow we will send an inquiry to Stella Baird."

John wasn't so sure.

Chapter 4

"How are you feeling today?" said Stella as she entered the room carrying a tray. "Breakfast's ready," she said pleasantly.

Thomas had been recovering well. He could tell the wound was beginning to heal and he had regained limited movement of his shoulder. Stella had taken good care of him although he felt she was mothering him a bit. He was ready to get out of bed and be on the go again, but she had thus far restrained him with her orders.

"I'm doing quite well, thank you. Well enough to be up and about I believe."

"I'm not so sure about that." Stella said, doubting his diagnosis. "It has only been ten days. I think you should take it easy for another week."

"I need to get up and get on my way. I have gold to find." Thomas said.

"You think so? And how do you propose to do that when you don't own a thing?"

"Well I intend to find out who robbed me and get my money back," Thomas said confidently.

"I'm afraid it won't be easy."

"Why?"

"Rumor has it, the man who shot and robbed you left town on the *North Wind* the day after you went down."

Thomas sat up in bed. "You mean you know who did this to me?"

Stella sat the tray down on the bedside table. She had been avoiding this topic for several days, ever since word had gone around town about the robbery. It pained her to think people could treat other human beings with such disregard. The shooter apparently had a few too many the night of the crime and bragged to a fellow partaker about his new found wealth and his plans to leave the following afternoon. Rumors swirled wildly until some of the local boys came and told Stella.

"No—only rumors," she said.

"Well, tell me!" Thomas said, growing impatient.

"Some are saying it was Pierce."

"Samuel Pierce?" said Thomas. *It couldn't have been him, or could it?*, thought Thomas as he recalled their conversation on the ship.

"Pierce has been around and rumor is he killed a man during his trip to the Klondike, but there was never any proof. He has been known to shirk on his bills. Last time he left here owing me money for room and board. I think he has joined the ranks of those mining the miners, although I never would have thought him capable of shooting anyone."

"Last I saw him he was walking away as I was leaving the ship. He had a bottle in one hand," said Thomas.

Stella thought for a moment. "Maybe he got drunk and stupid enough to take a shot at you. We may never know for sure. Now eat your breakfast."

"I can't believe he would shoot me," said Thomas naively. "At this point it doesn't matter who did it; what matters is I'm stuck here without anything to my name."

"Well, you have a breakfast. Now eat it before it gets cold and I get mad," Stella said as she closed the door behind her.

Thomas swung his feet over the edge of the bed. It felt good to sit up. He slowly rotated his shoulder and winced in pain. It was stiff and sore but he could move it. *What a mess I'm in now.* He reached for the tray, thinking about how good Stella had been to him and wondering how he would repay her. Quite a contrast he thought, the good and evil together in this land. *I will have to be careful from now on.*

* * *

The following day dawned bright and clear, adding to Thomas' frustration at being stuck in a bed. He hoped to convince Stella he was well enough to at least begin a more active routine.

"I think I'm ready to get out and about," he said as Stella entered the room with her tray of bandages and ointments.

"I'm not so sure about that young man."

"Well, I have to do something other than lay around all day."

"Take your shirt off and let me check that hole in you to see how it's healing," she said as she sat the tray down next to the bed.

Thomas complied as Stella carefully watched his movements while removing the shirt.

"You look a little sore still, judging by the way you wiggled out of your shirt."

"It hurts a bit, but nothing I can't stand."

"Let's take a look," she said as she began peeling back the old dressing. "Well, looks like it's healed up enough where it won't start bleeding again, if you don't overdo. Now lift your arm and move it around to work the shoulder some."

Thomas slowly lifted his left arm above his head, being careful to hide any indication of pain. He moved it around and realized that although it didn't hurt much when he was sitting still, moving it was a different matter.

"Okay, you're going to need to wear a sling for a while."

"I don't need it. I'm fine."

"No, I insist. If you're going to be up and about you're going to wear a sling for at least a few days."

Thomas realized arguing was pointless, noting it would be impossible to disagree with the advice of "Doctor" Stella. Thomas smiled as she fussed over him, putting on new bandages, then helping him on with his shirt and adjusting the sling she had fashioned in anticipation.

"What are you smiling about?" she demanded.

"Oh nothing, just enjoying the morning," Thomas said with a bit of the devil in his eye.

"All right Mr. Thomas, but you just watch your step with me," she said, trying to maintain her air of authority. "So what do you have planned?"

"Well I want to send word to Emily and let her know I'm doing fine. Also I need to find work so I can get on with my prospecting. Oh, and one more thing, if I ever run across Pierce again, he'll have some fast talking to do."

"That's quite a bit of planning for your first day," said Stella, smiling at him. "As for Pierce, he's long gone. I think you better take it easy for a few more days before you go venturing off to town."

"But I need to get a letter off to Emily."

"Tell you what, you write it and I'll flag down one of the wagons going to town and make sure it gets delivered."

"I'm pretty sure I can make it to town and back."

"Well I'm not. A few more days recovery won't hurt you any. You don't want to mess up my work on your shoulder now, do you?"

"Okay, if you insist," Thomas said reluctantly. He knew she was right but he was getting antsy from just sitting around.

"As for work, it could be hard to find. Honest work doesn't pay much here. It's the suppliers and merchandisers that are making the money," Stella said. "Your best bet would be to sign on with somebody headed to the gold fields. Maybe work for someone on a claim for a year or so till you get a grubstake."

"I didn't come here to work for other people." Thomas said sarcastically. "The only reason I will take on a job is to get enough money to move on."

"Don't you have somebody down south that could grubstake you?" Stella asked. She had seen a lot of people pass through and she knew how difficult it was to make a go of it when starting from scratch.

"Well, my mother has just enough to live on. I couldn't take any from her."

"What about Emily?" said Stella.

"I wouldn't ask Emily or her parents for money. I want to make my own way," he said, his pride poking through.

"Just asking," said Stella. "It doesn't hurt to consider all your options. It's going to be tough on you until your shoulder gets back into shape."

"I know. I guess I'll just have to take things as they come."

"Tell me about this Emily of yours," said Stella.

"Well, she is a beautiful young woman," said Thomas, a faint smile spreading across his face.

"Surely there is more to her than that."

"Of course," said Thomas. "She is everything I had hoped for, but I worry I may be beneath her. You see, she comes from money and I'm just a poor farm boy from the East."

"So that's why you've come here—to seek your fortune so you are worthy of her?"

Thomas was taken back a bit by her bluntness, causing him to question his true motives. "That's a big part of it. Truth be known I do have a small case of gold fever, but she's the real reason."

"If her family has any common sense they will look beyond your background. You seem like a nice young man to me, even though you don't listen to your doctor very well."

"I hope you're right. I know her mother has high expectations for Emily and wants her to marry well."

"Have you asked for her hand?"

"I have, but we won't marry until I can prove I can provide for her. That's why I need to get a grubstake and head to the Interior."

"I understand. What is her father like?"

"He's a practical man. I like him and I like to think he likes me as well. He started with pretty much nothing and made his fortune as a land developer."

"A self-made man. Where does his business take him? Just the Seattle area?"

"Oh, no. He sold off his business several years ago and they live off their investments."

"Ah," said Stella. "So they are *very* well off."

"Yes. I have a lot to live up to," said Thomas.

"Don't put too heavy a load on your shoulders. If it's meant to be her parents will accept you for who you are."

"Maybe," said Thomas, looking quite uncertain.

"How did you and Emily meet?"

"Quite by accident," said Thomas. "I was working

the docks unloading cargo when Emily and her father happened along. He had purchased a grand piano for her from back East and they were there to ensure it made it safely from the ship to shore."

"A grand piano? Was it for a special occasion?"

"No, she had wanted one for a long time and her father finally obliged. I hope you don't think she is spoiled."

"Not yet. Please continue," said Stella as she crossed her arms and smiled.

"Well, a large container of goods was being swung from a ship over the dock as Emily was following her father down the walkway. Suddenly there was a loud crack as one of the straps broke and the container shifted. I was standing nearby and rushed forward, grabbing Emily by the waist and swinging her out of harm's way. I managed to jump back just as the container hit the dock and smashed to pieces."

"Oh, my," said Stella. "So you saved her life."

"I guess you could say so. She was quite shaken and her father couldn't thank me enough. We talked for a bit, Emily not saying much, and her father tried to pay me for rescuing her—which of course I refused. It was then he insisted I come to their house for dinner the following Sunday."

"So you went?"

"Yes, I wavered back and forth but finally put on the best clothes I had and went. Especially since I agreed to go when first invited. It turned out to be the best decision I have ever made. They invited me to church and I went because of Emily. We grew close from then on, even though I'm pretty sure her mother still doesn't completely approve."

"Sounds like Sunday dinner from that point on," said

Stella.

"Yes, we spent a lot of time together; always properly chaperoned of course. Enough of this chatter; now it's time for me to get out of this room. Come on downstairs and I'll buy you a cup of coffee."

"Buy me a cup of coffee? You don't have any money."

"I know," Thomas said with a grin.

* * *

"But we must go, we simply must!" Emily was pleading with her parents. "He needs me, he might be dying!" she said, tears welling up in her big blue eyes.

John Palmer glanced quickly at Lydia, then said to Emily, "It's far too dangerous Emily. We will send a telegram or letter to Miss Baird. I promise you I will find out how Thomas is doing."

He knew that Emily wouldn't like the answer but he felt it was best and he must reason with her.

"If we left now, today, it would be a week or two before we could reach Valdez. That's if we could even get passage on such short notice. While we are on our way, Thomas might send word and we would miss it. Worse yet, he might even now be on his way back and we certainly wouldn't want to pass him on the high seas."

"I hadn't thought of it that way," Emily said, wiping the tears. "Perhaps you are right, I hope he is on his way home right now!"

"If we haven't heard from him in a month or so, I promise, we will take further measures," said John, much to the chagrin of his wife.

Later that day Emily and her father made a trip to the telegraph office, only to learn that the lines to Valdez were down, the poles toppled by heavy winter storms.

Although they were working on repairs, the clerk couldn't tell them when service would be restored. Emily was devastated by the news, knowing that she would now have to wait even longer to hear from Thomas.

They made their way to the post office, where they mailed a brief letter to Stella Baird inquiring about Thomas, whether he was still there, and how he was doing. Emily had asked how long it would take for the letter to get there. The man across the counter chuckled and said "One can never tell, young lady."

Emily realized that it might be six weeks, maybe two months before she knew of Thomas' fate. It wasn't going to be easy to wait.

* * *

Later that day, Thomas wrote a letter to Emily:

My Dearest Emily,

As you know I came to some misfortune when I first arrived in Valdez. Miss Stella is taking good care of me and I am recovering well. My shoulder is still a little sore but should be in good shape in a week or two. All my money is gone but do not be concerned, I will be able to find work soon.

Please take care of yourself and don't worry about me. I will write you again once I have found work. Greet your parents for me.

Love,

Thomas

Chapter 5

Laying back in bed, Thomas reflected on his situation. He had recovered to the point where he had to get out and do something. He was tired of being nursemaided by Stella, despite the fact he fully appreciated it and could never repay her kindness. He simply had to find work, earn some money, and then get to the Interior.

Yet, in the back of his mind he was worried, overwhelmed. *Have I taken too big of a risk? Am I up to the challenges?* The last thing he ever imagined was being destitute in the middle of nowhere—he had taken such care to come prepared and now...

Stella's voice snapped him back to attention.

"Breakfast's ready and I'm not bringing it to you in bed anymore," she said, cheerfully calling to him from downstairs.

Thomas eased out of bed and dragged himself into the dining room. Stella's other boarders were already gone for the day—they came and went quickly as each new group of dreamers headed out to seek their fortune. Slipping into the high-back chair, Thomas surveyed the room.

In what might be considered typical Alaska fashion, the decor consisted of antiques and pictures strategically placed around the room. Rusty traps hung from a bronze hook in the corner. On the high wall above the fireplace hung an impressive moose rack with bleached skull.

The adjacent wall sported a large brown bear rug. Thomas thought meeting such a creature in the wild must be more than a bit frightening. On the wall behind him was a head mount of a full curl Dall sheep. His curiosity grew as he surveyed the trophies.

The photograph of a somewhat grizzled man sporting a large caliber rifle next to numerous sheep, bears, moose, and wolves made Thomas wonder about the man.

"Here's your breakfast," Stella said as she placed a large plate of eggs, fried potatoes, and steak in front of Thomas.

Thomas dug in eagerly—he didn't realized how hungry he was and this was his first big meal since being shot.

"Hmm, good steak. I'll bet beef costs plenty here."

"It does, and it's not. It's moose."

"Moose? Well it's fine by me!" said Thomas as he hacked off another big chunk. "Aren't you going to eat anything?"

"I ate earlier," Stella said as she headed off to the kitchen to fetch the coffee.

She returned with a steaming cup, placed it in front of Thomas, and sat down across from him. Thomas looked up.

"So tell me about the trophies. Where did they come from?"

Stella's eyes seemed to sadden as she looked down at the table. Thomas quickly realized he must have struck a nerve.

"I'm sorry. I didn't mean to pry."

"It's okay," Stella said quietly. "It's still a bit difficult for me even after all this time."

Stella shifted in her chair, composed herself and looked straight at Thomas.

"All these trophies were taken by my husband. He was a wonderful man and a great hunter," Stella said matter-of-factly.

With that, Stella began to tell the story of her husband Wesley Baird—and his disappearance.

Chapter 6

"Absolutely not!" exclaimed Lydia, standing over John and Emily, hands on her hips, her voice fuming. "Neither of you are going to Alaska!"

A fitful nights sleep did little to change Emily's mind. She wanted to be with Thomas, to care for him, to nurse him back to health. In her mind sending a letter and waiting forever for another in return was no solution. Throughout the night she had rolled it over and over in her mind how she would convince her father to take her to Alaska.

Her early morning pleading had easily convinced him. He wanted to go with Thomas in the first place but never voiced it, knowing the reaction his wife would surely have. Plus he was hampered by the often stifling bondage of those in upper society; that need to carry on properly. His family was well cared for and he viewed this plan as an opportunity to return to something he longed for—adventure and a sense of accomplishment.

"Taking a nineteen-year-old girl to the wilds of Alaska is irresponsible." Lydia continued. "I for the life of me can't understand what you are thinking John."

"I'll be twenty in two months," Emily blurted out as tears began to well up in her eyes.

John had anticipated his wife's reaction and had carefully plotted his response. Settling into the plush leather chair of the sitting room, he slowly and deliberately took his pipe and tobacco and lit it. The fragrant smoke drifted up slowly, building anticipation in the air.

"Lydia, I believe you aren't thinking this through carefully," said John.

"How so?"

"Emily, would you mind if your mother and I had a

few words alone?" said John, prompting Emily to quietly retreat from the sitting room, gently closing the ornate wooden door as she left.

"First of all, think of your poor daughter," said John. "She has been on edge since Thomas left and practically inconsolable since we heard from Alaska. Frankly I'm concerned about her health."

"I have noticed she hasn't been eating much and she certainly is weepy," Lydia admitted. "But I'm afraid John."

"I think it is best we go and find Thomas and hopefully convince him to come home with us. It sounds like he is in no condition to continue on to the gold fields," said John. "It will be perfectly safe," he continued. "And I will ask Preston to look in on you. If you need anything he will take care of it for you while I'm gone."

Preston Van Sant and John had served together in the army. He was also their lawyer and looked after their financial interests. John considered him a loyal and faithful friend.

"How long would you be gone?" asked Lydia, still skeptical.

"We would be as quick as possible. Emily needs to see this through, but I certainly don't intend to go chasing the young man all across Alaska," answered John.

"Go if you must, but I think it is unfair for me to be the one waiting now."

"Don't worry, we will send word back with the boat and I will write every few days to keep you updated," said John.

"When will you leave?"

"As soon as I can arrange it," he said, neglecting to tell her he had already asked Preston to book passage for them on a steamer leaving in two weeks time.

Chapter 7

With sadness in her eyes Stella told the story of her and Wesley. They had grown up in the same little town in Montana. Early on she had caught his eye and by the time they were in their late teens it was apparent to everyone they would marry.

After the wedding, Wesley worked odd jobs here and there but never really found his calling. He gently began to mention going north and all the opportunities waiting for those brave enough to venture forth. Stella had some reservations about leaving home and family, but having migrated from the Dakotas to Montana with her family as a young girl the idea wasn't foreign to her. Wesley worked on her for nearly a year until she warmed to the idea and said yes.

They arrived in Alaska long before the masses now traversing the land. Wes had dreams of gold mining in the summer and trapping in the winter. He wasn't a hard rock miner but preferred to placer mine the rich gravels using a sluice box and shovel. It was grueling work and after several short summers and long winters they were still struggling.

Working the ground by hand was back-breaking work and Wes realized he just couldn't move enough gravel to make it pay, even with hired help. The claim was in a narrow canyon and couldn't be worked easily by any other method. Though they brought in a bit of gold each year, it was just enough to cover expenses and put a little away.

After some debate, they decided to sell the mining claim and put up a boarding house. It was largely Stella's idea and while not wanting to quash Wes' dream, she convinced him it would give them a much better life. Wes had agreed and they built the boarding house out of town, strategically placed on the route to the Interior. Once in operation, Wes found there was little for him to do. Stella managed the whole thing nicely except for the occasional maintenance task. Rather than sit back and take it easy, Wes saw an opportunity—market hunting.

The demand for fresh meat was great and the cost of importing beef and chicken was outrageous. With the abundant wildlife in the area, hunting and supplying the local eatery and general store with fresh meat would provide a tidy profit. Wes had brought a couple of rifles to Alaska with them—a Winchester Model 1876 and the .45-70 Government. His favorite was the Winchester and he used it almost exclusively.

Wes would be gone several days at a time, taking two pack horses into the backcountry and returning loaded down with moose, Dall sheep, or the occasional black bear. Between the boarding house, hunting, and the winter trapline, Stella and Wesley were finally doing well. Their business grew and soon any thoughts of gold mining vanished from their minds.

Stella paused and took a deep breath. "I didn't think it would be hard for me to tell this story, but it still is," she said quietly.

"I'm sorry," said Thomas. "Don't feel like you have to tell me; I didn't mean to upset you."

"No, I want to tell you," Stella said, clutching her hands together in her lap as she continued.

"It was late September, the leaves had started to turn and the nights were getting cold enough to leave a light frost. It was Wes' favorite time of year."

He loved the smell of the woods, the crisp sharp mornings and the thrill of the hunt. The moose were entering rut and easier to hunt. With the urge to reproduce, the

strongest bulls assembled harems of cow moose and vig-
orously defended against all challengers. In their love
induced craze, they threw caution to the wind, making
them easy to stalk.

"I really looked forward to this time of year," said
Stella. "I was able to put up a fair amount of food for the
winter from our small garden and we smoked meats we
needed to get us through the long winter."

Stella recalled the last day she saw him. Wes packed
the two horses, kissed Stella goodbye, and said "See you
in three days." Five days later one of the horses wan-
dered back into town, barren of its pack. Stella had been
worried on day four and when the horse returned she
descended into a state of panic. Something was clearly
wrong.

"Some of the men in town assembled a search party
to look for him," said Stella.

No one was sure where Wes went—like many hunters
he held his "spots" close to the vest. This made it difficult
to search, but over a period of ten days they scoured the
known game trails and valleys. On the third of October
the snow began to fall and the search was over. No sign
of Wes or the other horse was ever found.

"That was five years ago," she said.

Some in town suggested Wes had disappeared on purpose, slipping out of town on a steamer and heading south.
Those that knew him quickly dismissed the thought. Besides, there was no way he could sneak out of town un-
noticed—everyone knew him.

"I was devastated," said Stella. "It was a very long
winter, the darkness and cold only made my loneliness
worse."

Some had tried to convince her she should leave; return to her family in Montana. She declined, perhaps

somehow holding out a faint glimmer of hope that some-day Wes would be found.

"I still miss him," she said. "Not knowing what happened to him pains me every day."

"I'm truly sorry Stella," Thomas said. He wished he could comfort her but was at a loss for words. He marveled at how strong a woman she was and yet how vulnerable.

"He would be proud of you. You're are truly a strong woman," Thomas said.

"Thank you," she said. "I'm so glad you are here; you've been great company to me, even though you haven't been much help," she said, grinning.

The mood lightened and Thomas breathed a sigh of relief. Stella's composure returned and she announced "Time for coffee!" as she scurried off to the kitchen.

As the smell of freshly brewing coffee drifted in from the kitchen, Thomas formulated a plan; but he had to approach it delicately. Listening to Stella made him wonder about his options for making some money so he could move on to the gold fields. He tried in vain to come up with a clever way to broach the topic so when Stella returned with coffee he blundered forward.

"Stella, what would you think if we entered into a partnership?"

"I hope you aren't proposing to me mister because you are way too young," she said briskly.

Thomas laughed, "No, a business partnership."

"What do you have in mind?"

Thomas hesitated, his eyes shifting to the floor.

"Well?" she said, staring directly at him.

"I was thinking maybe I could take up hunting. We could sell to the eateries, miners, and the general store and split the profits."

Stella stared at him. The seconds ticked by and Thomas regretted bringing it up at all. He should have waited a day or two after hearing her story.

"You know I told you it pains me every day to think of what happened to Wes," she began. "But you know what, we have to go on. I miss him dearly and yet we both knew the risks of living in this wild land. If you want to hunt, I'll support you—but I can't help worrying about you at the same time," she said.

"I'll be fine," Thomas said, knowing the words sounded more like pride than confidence.

"Do you know anything at all about guns? Or hunting?" Stella asked.

"I was the best shot in the whole county back home," Thomas said, pretending to be insulted.

"How about bears? Big bears?"

"Well we have black bears but not the big grizzly bears. I'm not worried too much about them," said Thomas, trying to put on an air of confidence.

Stella looked at him and smiled. She liked him. He was young, ambitious, and a bit brash, but she knew he was a good man.

"Here is the deal. I have a pack horse and I still have the .45-70 and enough cartridges to get you started. Do you think your shoulder is up to it?"

Thomas placed his hand on his left shoulder and rotated it as if to illustrate. The burning pain that shot through to the middle of his back was not enough to make him wince. "Yes, I'm up to it."

"Okay then, I guess we have a deal. I'll back you with equipment and we'll share in the profits. I have some other things you'll need too, some pack frames and other camping gear that belonged to Wes."

"That sounds great," said Thomas. "I can't wait to get started."

As Stella cleared the coffee and returned to the kitchen she thought, *I hope I'm doing the right thing.*

* * *

Thomas was excited. At last he could see some progress. Even though it still pained him, his shoulder was feeling better, and now, thanks to Stella, he could get out and start replenishing his grubstake.

Stella was well known and respected in town. She could easily talk the local establishments into buying any wild game that was brought their way. In a way, Thomas felt a bit guilty; everything was being handed to him and he had done nothing in return. He vowed that would soon change.

After three days of sunning himself on the porch, taking in the early spring scenery, Thomas made plans to venture out of the boarding house. He wanted to get some information on where he should start his hunting efforts.

Stella was finishing up the breakfast dishes when Thomas entered the kitchen.

"I'd like to go into town today and talk to some folks about hunting areas."

"That might be worthwhile, but I'll warn you, people around here are going to be tight-lipped when it comes to revealing their hunting spots."

"Surely they can give me some idea?"

"They'll talk alright. You'll get vague generalities and lots of hand waving. If you're lucky you might even get a fact or two from the conversations. I'd start with Noel at the general store and see what he has to say."

"That's fine with me. I'll take any information I can get." Thomas knew there would be lots of hard work and long hours ahead of him if he was to make a go of it.

"You know how to ride a horse?" asked Stella.

"Sure, you forget I was raised on a farm," said Thomas.

"Come with me," she said, heading for the back door. Thomas dutifully followed her to the barn.

"This is the only horse I have left. She's a good old gal and works hard. Be nice to her."

"Of course," said Thomas.

Stella pointed out where the saddle, blanket, and bit where stored and stepped back to see if Thomas knew what to do with them.

"Saddle her up," she said.

Thomas took the blanket and tossed it on, then set the saddle gently on the back of the horse. Immediately she puffed out her stomach a bit, using a trick all horses seem to know. Thomas paused, then gave her a bit of knee just under the ribs and cinched the saddle tight. For a split second he questioned how to make the cinch knot, but it came back to him quickly. He finished up by securing the bridle and bit and stepped back to admire his handiwork.

The horse was a stocky animal and looked like she had a bit of Morgan in her. He bet she could handle herself on the hunting grounds.

"Not bad," said Stella. "I see she didn't fool you with her little trick."

"See, I told you I'd been around horses," said Thomas smiling.

"Well, point her down the road and give her rein. She'll take you right to town."

"Thanks," said Thomas as he led the horse from the barn and mounted up. The horse paused for a moment and then started down the road without any prodding.

"Told you," said Stella as she waved. "Be careful."

Thomas let the horse do the work while he took in the scenery on the way to town. This was his first real look at the terrain, since on his first trip to the boarding house he was unconscious. The day was bright and he enjoyed the leisurely ride, looking at each valley and wondering what lay beyond.

Following Stella's suggestion, his first stop was the general store. She had told Thomas about Noel Parker, how he had been there for ten years, starting the store early in the gold rush and making a decent living. He had a charming wife and a couple of rambunctious nine year old twin boys that could often be found bouncing around the store. Noel was tall, a quiet and honest man. Honesty was a valued commodity in a gold rush town—there was usually little to be found.

Thomas pushed the creaky door open and stopped, his eyes widening. The store was crammed to the seams with goods of all kind. *There must have been a ship in recently for the store to be so full*, he thought.

While overflowing, the store was clean, with rough wooden floors and a large counter backed by shelves of canned goods, tools, and everything else one might need on the frontier. Large crosscut saws hung from the rafters, the kind that took two men to operate. Snowshoes, traps, and coils of rope rounded out the decor. There were no prices marked on anything. Thomas guessed they changed daily and everyone likely understood the principles of a frontier marketplace.

Thomas stepped forward and extended his hand to the man behind the counter. "I'm Thomas Thornton," he said, shaking the man's hand.

"Noel Parker. Pleased to meet you. Stella tells me

you're going to do some hunting for us."

"That's right," said Thomas. "I'm hoping you can give me some help getting started."

"Well, I'm not much of a hunter, but I do know a spot you might try. Nobody goes there," said Noel.

"Why not?"

"Well, it's rough country. A high hanging valley that is real hard to get into. I think there's a big glacier at the head of the valley. Rumors are the critters are plentiful."

"Nobody else hunts it?"

"Not that I know of. Some have thought about it, but they have other spots that are easier to get to. Here, let me mark a couple others for you on this here map," Noel said as he reached for a folded map and laid it out on the wooden counter.

Thomas watched eagerly as Noel marked four or five spots on the map. He wasn't sure how Noel knew of these places, but assumed it was by talking with customers.

"And this here is Goat Creek, the rough one I told you about," Noel said.

Thomas looked at the map. Goat Creek was several miles from town and, to him, it didn't look like it was that tough of a go. Thomas didn't really care where he went, as long as he could find game and not trespass on someones so-called private hunting reserve. He resolved to check out Goat Creek first.

"You need any supplies or anything? I got plenty of cartridges and most other gear you're gonna need."

"No, Stella has me pretty much outfitted to the hilt. But I'm sure we'll be doing business in the future."

Thomas thanked Noel as he turned to leave. "What do I owe you for the map?" he asked.

"Keep it," said Noel.

Thomas stepped out of the store and glanced up the street at the saloon. *Sure a lot of horses and wagons there for early afternoon*, he thought.

He walked the short distance to the saloon and entered, immediately being struck by the strong smell of tobacco and stale beer. His eyes narrowed as he tried to adjust to the darkness.

There was a small crowd sitting around tables and at the bar, talking loudly over each other.

"What'll you have?" yelled the bartender, motioning for Thomas to come forward.

"Nothing thanks," said Thomas as he approached the bar.

The bartender frowned and growled, "Gotta drink or gotta leave. Your choice."

"What's a matter? You a teetotaler?" yelled a drunk from the end of the bar.

Thomas wasn't interested in spending the few dollars Stella had lent him in this manner, but decided if he wanted information he had to play along.

"Give me a beer," he said.

The bartender drew a beer and slammed the mug down, slopping the stale smelling brew on the bar. "Two bits," he said.

Thomas reluctantly paid up, and slid the beer to the side.

"What? You too good to drink with us?" said the drunk as he approached Thomas.

Thomas ignored him, glancing towards the exit.

"Answer me boy," said the drunk, poking a finger hard into Thomas' sore shoulder.

Thomas swung around, his good fist raised and ready to strike.

"Back off Billy. Go sit down or I'm running you out of here---again," said the bartender.

Billy, swore under his breath and staggered back, retreating to his bar stool.

"Sorry mister," said the bartender.

Thomas put his fist down and didn't answer. *This is pointless*, he thought, realizing he wasn't going to get anything worthwhile here. The last thing he needed was a fight. Pushing back from the bar, he headed for the door.

"Hey, you didn't drink your beer," shouted the bartender.

Without looking back, Thomas raised his hand and swept it down to his side as he pushed out the door, stepping into the bright sunlight.

He resolved to do this the hard way—check out Goat Creek and if it didn't pan out, he'd explore as far as needed to find his own hunting grounds.

On the long ride back to the boarding house, his thoughts drifted towards Seattle and the girl he had left behind. He missed her, but yet he had prepared himself before he left, knowing it could be a long time before they held each other again. He wished he could see her now, to share with her all that had happened.

As he neared the boarding house the sun began to set, the clouds hanging low on the horizon. As the bright oranges and reds began their slow dance into night, Thomas hoped Emily was well.

Chapter 8

The *S.S. Spokane* rolled back and forth, wallowing in the swells that continued to flow in from the west. She was the finest ship in the Pacific Coast Steamship Company fleet. At 270 feet long she could carry 171 first-class passengers in comfortable accommodations and had facilities for another hundred in steerage.

The *Spokane* was designed for the excursion trade that had sprung up in the wake of the gold rush. In addition to tourists, she regularly carried miners and cannery workers as well as cargo.

None of this mattered to Emily. The weather had turned foul and now the rollers were pushing ten feet in height, with an occasional wave breaking over the bow of the ship, making the ride anything but smooth.

"I don't think I can take much more of this, Father," said Emily. "I feel like I am going to be sick again."

It had been an agonizing two weeks for Emily, from the time they had decided to come to Alaska until the ship departed. The days dragged by, each the same, filled with worry and uncertainty. She thought continually of Thomas, imagining the worst and hoping for the best.

The day of departure finally arrived, Father and her waving goodbye to Mother from the bow of the ship as it slipped its mooring and steamed away.

She was glad to be on the way and the trip from Seattle had been uneventful—until they had left the protection of the islands and entered open water. There the huge rolling waves rocked the ship, sending many a passenger to the rail in agony.

Emily was so pale; just looking at her caused John's stomach to knot up tight. With each passing day he questioned the decision to bring her to Alaska.

"Only a few more days dear and we will arrive," he said, with thin hope of comforting her. "It will be worth it when we get there."

"I know, but I am so miserable at times."

"Let's see if we can get some tea. Maybe that will help settle your stomach; and we can talk about all the things we will do as soon as we get to Alaska."

They retired to the galley and ordered some tea. The ship didn't have much in the way of amenities, but it did offer the basics needed to keep the passengers moderately comfortable during the voyage.

"Here we go," said John as the steward brought them their tea. "This will help."

"I hope so Father," said Emily. "How much longer before we arrive?"

"I am not exactly sure dear; it depends on the weather, but it should be within three or four days," John said, trying not to reveal it could be twice that long.

"I guess I can make it that long. I can't wait to see Thomas."

"Hopefully we will be able to find him easily since we know where he is staying. The question is, what do we do after we find him?" said John.

"What do you mean?"

"Well, what do you hope will happen?"

"He will come back to Seattle with us, of course," said Emily confidently.

"Are you so sure? I mean he was so determined to make his fortune."

"I will make him come back with us," she said with an air of certainty in her voice.

"And if he refuses?"

Emily looked down into her tea cup and suddenly realized her plans might not align with what Thomas had in mind.

"After all, we only came to make sure he was fine and see if we could help him, not force him to return with us," said her father.

Emily stared out the window as the ship continued to roll in the swells. A rain squall was pattering the window, the drops running down in long streaks, mirroring the tears welling up in her eyes.

"Everything will be fine—you'll see. Now drink your tea," said John.

Everything will be fine, he told himself. He just hoped this trip was not a mistake, that he could protect Emily from whatever lay before them, and they would find Thomas. They had come with sufficient funds to stay for a while if need be.

Deep down in his heart John would like to stay as long as possible, to do some exploring and recapture the sense of adventure that had evaporated with his youth. *Lydia would not be happy, but she seldom was*, John thought, quickly regretting his attitude towards his wife. She had become so entrenched in Seattle society and the stuffiness it bred he hardly knew her anymore. He longed for the playfully innocent young woman he had been attracted to long ago.

In the long run he would do the right thing—balance the needs of his daughter with the demands of his wife.

They finished their tea and returned to their stateroom, such as it was. *Emily seems to be feeling better,* he thought.

"Get some rest now dear," he said. "I'm sure you'll feel much better in the morning."

"Thank you Father. And thank you for allowing me

to go and find Thomas."

"You're welcome Emily, you're welcome," he said, pushing aside the doubts and fears that lay before him.

Chapter 9

Thomas woke before dawn, the anticipation of the hunt driving him to get an early start. The night before he had gone through all the gear Stella had provided. He arranged his packsack carefully, making sure he had all the provisions he would need for a day trip: matches, some food, an extra pair of gloves, hunting knife, and a small hatchet. Yet he lacked one important item—a rifle.

Stella had held back the rifle and cartridges, even though Thomas asked about them a number of times. Finally she explained she wanted to present them to him formally as he departed on his first hunt. Thomas thought formality a bit odd in a place like this, but he played along. He suspected it had more to do with giving up a part of Wesley than it did a "formal presentation."

He would have preferred to have the rifle ahead of time so he could get used to it and run a few rounds through it, but he would have plenty of time to do it on this trip. After all, Thomas didn't expect much his first time out. He didn't know the country and this was more of a scouting mission than an actual hunt. If he was fortunate and came across a moose or sheep, so much the better. He wished there were deer around but they inhabited the surrounding islands, not the mainland. Moose and sheep would be his goal.

Thomas dressed quickly, grabbed his bag and headed downstairs to the dining room. Stella was busy in the kitchen. The coffee was on and the smell of bacon, biscuits in the oven, and gravy simmering away filled the air. He loved her cooking.

As Thomas dropped his bag next to the table, Stella turned from her work, her free hand flying to her cheek. "My, you're up early."

"I am on a mission today," Thomas said with a broad smile.

"Well you must be raring to go to be up this early; it's not even daylight."

"By the time I have seconds or thirds of that breakfast I'll have plenty of light."

"You eat that much you won't be able walk, let alone climb that hill you've got in mind," said Stella.

Stella had a few boarders renting rooms but most had moved on. She still had to get up early and get things ready for those leaving today and the next batch of transients needing a room that night. Thomas wondered if she ever slept.

"Your breakfast will be ready in a few minutes. Since you're up so early you can eat before the others get out of bed," she said.

"Good, I want to get going early."

Stella turned and gave him the eye. She worried his exuberance would lead to misfortune.

"Now remember, Alaska is a wild and dangerous place. You step outside off the porch and you better be ready to survive," Stella said, exaggerating to try to get her point across. "A lot of greenhorns have come up here and got in plenty of trouble. I want you to be careful," she said, biting her lip.

She liked Thomas, had begun to think of him as the son she never had; and with Wesley ever in the back of her mind, she was worried about him. The dangers were many and varied and she knew them all: avalanches, river crossing, crevasses, bears, and just plain exposure to the elements.

"Don't worry, I'll be fine," said Thomas confidently as he slid into a chair at the dining room table.

Stella plopped down a big plate of biscuits and gravy with a nice helping of bacon in front of Thomas. A steaming cup of coffee rounded out the meal.

Thomas ate with a sense of urgency, taking huge bites and wolfing it down.

"Slow down young man! Where are your manners?"

Thomas stopped in mid-chew, taken aback by Stella's sudden scolding.

"I'm sorry ma'am," he said, half smiling. "I'm just too excited to get going today. You know I've been cooped up in here for what seems like months!"

"I know. But you can still behave like a gentleman," she said, smiling a bit and easing the tension.

Thomas finished his meal, but slowly. Downing the last of his coffee, he placed the cup on the table and sat quietly, looking at Stella.

"Well, what are you waiting for? Get going!" said Stella.

"I think you are supposed to give me something this morning," Thomas said almost impatiently.

"Oh that," said Stella coyly.

Thomas knew she was messing with him, stalling just to make him a bit more antsy. Stella left the dining room. Thomas waited. After a several minutes he wondered if she was coming back. Just as he started to scoot his chair away to get up, she reappeared.

There were tears in her eyes. Thomas realized immediately what was going on. Fetching the rifle had brought back in vivid detail the pain of Wesley's disappearance. Stella slowly caressed the wood grain of the rifle stock, staring at it as she stood in the doorway. Thomas didn't say anything, but waited until she was ready to speak.

Without a word, she handed the .45-70 to Thomas

and left the room. Thomas stood there, wondering if that was it and he should leave. It felt a bit odd; he needed to talk to her to see if she was okay.

In a moment, Stella returned, a box in her hand and her eyes dried of tears. "Here are the cartridges you'll need. There should be enough there to keep you in business for a while."

"Are you sure you want to let me use the rifle?" Thomas said hesitantly.

"Yes, Thomas. I want you to use it. I know you'll treat it right; it still means a lot to me."

"I'll take good care of it. You can count on that."

"Stella," he began, "I want you to know how much this means to me, I jus—"

"That's enough blubbering," she said. "You better get packed up and get moving, you have a long day ahead of you."

Thomas set the rifle on the table, took the cartridges from her hands, and gave her a big hug.

"Now you get going. The horse is waiting on you," she said, ending the hug abruptly by smacking him firmly on the back.

"I'll bring you a moose," he said, as he grabbed up his gear and headed out the door.

"Just bring yourself back in one piece," she said. "That will be enough for today."

* * *

Thomas stepped off the porch and headed to the barn. Following his first experience with the horse, Thomas had asked about her name. Stella told him her name was "Horse." *Simple to remember*, he mused. Thomas

couldn't tell if Stella had a strong attachment to the animal, but truth be told it wasn't the first horse in the world
to carry that name. Thomas wondered if she would name
her dog, "Dog" and her cat, "Cat." Pets were a luxury
here; if you weren't a working animal there wasn't a lot
of use for you.

Thomas saddled up Horse and secured his gear. The
pain in his shoulder was bearable, as long as he kept it
loosened up. His movements were deliberate, using his
good arm to do the heavy lifting. Since the injury was to
his left shoulder it wouldn't have to bear the brunt of the
rifle's kick, if and when he fired it.

The saddle had a leather scabbard for the .45-70; one
that allowed you to quickly grab the rifle if the need
arose. With everything ready, he led the horse out of
the barn towards the road. Horse seemed to be ready for
the trip, not nervous a bit about what this new fellow had
in mind. Thomas mounted up, pointed Horse down the
road and started out. He glanced to his left and saw Stella
standing on the porch. She smiled and waved, a brief and
silent wave. He returned the gesture and gently urged the
horse along.

Looking at the map Noel had given him, it was about
two miles to the trailhead. From there it was another five
miles along the river until the trail ended. Once there,
Thomas would have to bust brush to begin his trip into
the Goat Creek valley.

Thomas smiled, occasionally whistling a little tune
as he rode along. The sun was just beginning to peak
over the mountains. Flocks of geese flew along the coast,
honking as they announced the annual trip north. It was
shaping up to be one of those warm spring days in Alaska.
Though there remained snow in places shaded from the
sun, the land was almost fully awake from its winter

slumber and man and animal alike were fully ready for it.

He reached the trailhead without incident and turned Horse on to the trail. Unlike the first part of the journey, the trail was narrow with rocks jutting out here and there. In places there was standing water from the spring runoff. Horse had no problem negotiating the trail. She was experienced in the Alaska wilderness and, as Thomas would soon learn, as comfortable busting thick brush as she was on a groomed street.

Thomas decided he should start to look for animal sign, since to this point he had been taking in the sights and doing a bit of daydreaming.

The explosion of brush happened suddenly on his left. Horse rared back and Thomas was almost thrown over backwards. His heart pounding he looked quickly to see four grouse winging their way between the tall spruce. He had surprised the grouse that were sitting just off the trail, causing them to erupt from the underbrush with what sounded like the coming of a freight train. Silence returned as the adrenaline faded from Thomas' system. *Whew, I thought it was a bear.*

It was a fortuitous event that snapped him back to reality. Thomas realized he hadn't loaded the gun; not a good idea in bear country. He went a bit further down the trail to a small meadow. Here he stopped, dismounted and let the horse graze a bit while he familiarized himself with the rifle.

He wanted to do this sooner, but of course Stella had kept the gun in reserve until the last minute. Thomas took it out of the scabbard and looked it over carefully. It was a lever action rifle, chambered in .45-70 Government. Thomas had never held one until today, but he knew of its history. The .45-70 had been established as the official cartridge of the U.S. Military in 1873. In 1886, Winchester introduced the lever action model that Thomas now held in his hands. It was a powerful weapon, albeit limited in range. Thomas would have to keep that in mind when the time came. He opened a box of cartridges and carefully loaded the rifle.

He wondered if Horse was comfortable with the sound of gunfire. Thomas wanted to test fire the rifle before he needed to use it for real. He tied off the reins to a small spruce and moved off twenty yards or so. He tore the flap from the cartridge box and stuck it on a twig close to the trunk of a two-inch spruce tree. Moving back about another thirty yards, Thomas dropped to one knee and took aim. Squeezing the trigger slowly rewarded him with a very unsatisfying click.

He had forgot to put a round in the chamber. *Its been a while,* he thought. Cycling the lever, Thomas chambered a round and took aim again. He squeezed the trigger. This time he was rewarded with a magnificent boom accompanied by a kick just below that of an angry mule. The flap from the box was gone and Thomas recovered from the recoil just in time to see the tree fall over, cut in two by the .45 caliber round. *That will do just fine.*

Thomas looked over at the horse and noted she didn't seem concerned at all with his antics. He placed the rifle in the scabbard, untied Horse, saddled up and continued on his way.

Two hours later he had reached the end of the trail. There was an old cabin here, long since abandoned, likely by a miner whose dreams along the river had failed to materialize. The cabin roof sagged in the middle, showing the stress from one too many winters of snow load. Other than that, it appeared to be in serviceable condition. The door was intact. Thomas thought about opening it up and investigating further but decided to reserve that for later. Instead, he pulled the map from his vest pocket and took a look.

Goat Creek was another mile or so upriver from the cabin. While it wasn't far, there was no trail. The terrain was dotted with a mixture of spruce, willow, and alder. The wetter areas were choked with thick willow and alder that seemed to form a wall. If that weren't enough, the undergrowth had a healthy mix of Devil's Club, a nasty plant with thorns an inch or more long. Between the thick growth, Devil's Club, and the swampy areas, Thomas quickly understood why no one went to Goat Creek.

As Thomas sat in the saddle, alternately staring at the map and the vegetation, Horse began to mosey towards the river. Thomas pulled back on the reins and stopped the horse, then returned to the map. A moment later, Horse headed towards the river again, this time ignoring the pressure on the reins as Thomas tried to stop her. *Maybe she wants a drink.* Thomas eased off the reins and Horse continued through the low brush towards the river. Clearing the brush, Thomas saw the river consisted of multiple channels with gravel bars, a typical braided river.

Before he could stop her, Horse ambled down the low bank to the river and began to cross the narrow braid. Thomas waited for her to stop and drink but she didn't. He began to grow impatient; he wanted to begin breaking trail, not fool around in the river with the horse. He pulled back on the reins, halting the horse mid-stream. As he tried to turn her back to shore, she snorted, shook her head up and down and forged ahead.

Thomas decided to give the horse rein and see what happened; at least for a moment or two. Horse crossed the small braid, reached the gravel bar and headed up-stream. The gravel bar that separated the two channels was fifty or sixty feet wide and extended a fair distance upstream. Thomas realized the horse wasn't as dim-witted as he thought. This was a way to make some progress towards Goat Creek without busting brush and slogging through swamps.

They continued upstream on the bar for about a quarter mile or so. Thomas was scanning the mountains that lined the valley, looking for Goat Creek. Noel had told Thomas that Goat Creek was in a hanging valley; a valley carved out by a mountain glacier. These typically started high up and looked like a normal valley, until you approached the mouth. Here the stream valley was cut off by the large glacier that once occupied the river channel, leaving a fairly steep drop off. To get into Goat Creek valley would require a climb out of the river channel; another reason why it was rarely if ever visited.

They rounded a bend in the river and Thomas was disappointed to see the gravel bar only went a short way before the stream channels became one. As he was contemplating what to do next, Horse suddenly veered left, crossed the shallow channel, and climbed the low bank. Before them was a wall of young spruce, no more than eight or ten feet high each, but so thick you couldn't see through it.

I guess that's the end of this route, thought Thomas. Just as he was about to pull the reins and turn the horse around, she put her head down and charged forward through the spruce wall. Thomas assumed this was an act of revenge for taking her from the comforts of home. She intended to wipe him off the saddle and leave him here. All he could do was hold on tight, pull his knees up and tuck his head down as close to her neck as possible. He closed his eyes as the young spruce branches slapped him in the face, stinging like hundreds of little needles. Then it was over; the stinging stopped and so did Horse. Thomas opened his eyes. Before him was a narrow trail leading up the side of the valley. It was lined with thick brush on both sides, but it was definitely a trail, *a man made trail*. It had been brushed out, but only minimally. The thick wall of young spruce served as a barrier to hide the trail from anyone traveling up the river.

As Horse headed up the trail, Thomas looked for signs of recent use. There were no fresh tracks and the alders had begun to reclaim the opening cut through it—no one had been here in a while.

* * *

The trail wound its way up the valley, through thick stands of alder and willow, occasionally skirting a small swamp here and there. Thomas estimated they had gone two miles from the spruce wall, steadily climbing in elevation. From the map he knew Goat Creek was a long glacial valley, extending almost seven miles from its confluence with the river.

The spruce trees became less frequent, the willow grew shorter and things began to open up as they climbed higher up the steep valley. Shortly, Thomas realized they had nearly reached timberline and the views opened up dramatically. They had successfully navigated the steep terrain of the hanging valley.

He wondered if this was good habitat for moose. The small feeder streams that came in from both sides of the valley were choked with stands of willow, probably eight to ten feet tall. Among the open areas of the slopes were stands of alder that looked like they might hold game. The creek was not huge but was a couple of feet deep and flowing rather quickly. For the first time today, Thomas pulled out his pocket watch and checked the time. *Nearly noon, time for lunch.* He found a spot near the creek with some decent fodder for Horse and dismounted.

So you know this place, eh old gal. Horse munched some low grass as Thomas pulled his pack down and looked around.

So far he had seen little sign of wild game. He had spent nearly six hours getting this far. There was still plenty of daylight left to explore a little further up the valley. Thomas found a large rock near the creek and sat down to enjoy the lunch Stella had so kindly packed for him. He was facing downstream, enjoying the view from the hanging valley looking down on the main river below.

Obviously it's no accident I made it this far, thought Thomas. This was Wesley's private hunting ground and Horse knew it well. She had guided Thomas here out of instinct. This only heightened Thomas' excitement. If Wesley had hunted here enough for the horse to know the way, it must be good ground.

Thomas finished the last bite of his lunch and began rummaging through his pack. He found the binoculars Stella had given him and pulled them out. He looked through them, twisting the knob to focus on the far slope. *I wonder how old these things are.*

They looked as though they had spent a lot of time in the field. Thomas turned them over and found a patent date stamped into the metal just behind the knob: 1872. *I bet these old glasses have seen a lot of things in their day,* thought Thomas. While old, it was clear they were far better than using the naked eye. Thomas began to glass the slopes, hoping to spot something in the open areas between the patches of alder.

The downside to hunting this time of year was the foliage. Moose can hide behind a single twig it seems—with the alder in full array it was nearly impossible to know where one might be. As he looked up the valley he saw that spring had not worked its magic all the way to the headwaters, snow still clinging to the slopes and in shaded draws. The higher up the valley he looked, the less the vegetation. Though the visibility was better, Thomas realized this meant there was nothing for the moose to eat.

After a half an hour of glassing and seeing nothing, Thomas decided to continue up the trail. He wanted to go as far as he could and still have time to head home before dark. He loaded up his gear and mounted up, making his way along the narrow trail towards the head of the valley.

Chapter 10

The *Spokane* steamed steadily northward towards the narrows. This was always a tense passage for the captain and crew. Enjoying the amenities aboard ship, the passengers had little knowledge of the danger that lie ahead.

The Wrangell Narrows was one of the most dangerous stretches of water along the Inside Passage. With twenty-two miles of winding, narrow channel, it required constant attention and careful maneuvering to avoid the rocks. While hazardous, the alternative was to sail the outside waters, fully exposed to the fury of the Pacific.

The captain had done this run many times before and was confident in his crew. As they approached the narrows, he placed a watchman on the bow and one on both the starboard and port sides of the ship. He ordered the ship slowed to a safe maneuvering speed and entered the narrows.

In good weather and daylight the buoys placed along the channel generally ensured safe passage. Today was not one of those days. It had been raining hard since early morning. The seas were choppy and the wind had steadily increased, blowing east to west across the narrows. The visibility continued to decrease as the clouds rolled in with the rain squalls.

For a moment, the captain had considered delaying passage through the narrows until the weather improved. He could anchor up in a nearby cove and wait it out, but then he likely would face complaints about the delay from some of the stuffier passengers. The *Spokane* wasn't a luxury ship, but it did have a fair number of first-class cabins occupied by wealthier passengers. The captain hated dealing with them. The passengers in steerage were much more pleasant than the wealthy and their high expectations. *No, a delay would cause more problems than proceeding,* he thought. He didn't need letters of complaint flowing into the company.

* * *

The ship slammed violently to a halt, throwing Emily to the floor of the dining room. Dishes flew from the tables and people grabbed for anything within reach to steady themselves. John managed to stay upright, but he wasn't sure how. People were screaming as panic set in.

"Emily!" her father shouted as he rushed to her side.

She wasn't moving and he could see blood seeping from a gash on her forehead. He knelt down and shook her gently. She moaned and slowly opened her eyes.

"Are you alright?"

Emily stirred, but didn't answer. Ignoring the panic around him, he focused only on his daughter. He gently sat her up.

"Emily?"

"Yes Father?"

"Are you alright?"

"My head hurts and I think I'm bleeding."

John examined the gash on her head. Fortunately, it looked worse than it was, but he was still concerned. He turned and found a nearby napkin and pressed it gently to her wound to stop the bleeding.

"Here, let's get you to a chair."

John helped Emily to her feet and sat her in the nearest chair. The panic began to subside somewhat as people picked themselves up off the floor. The silence of the engines and the lack of movement told the passengers something was seriously wrong.

* * *

The captain cursed as the blast of wind forced the *Spokane* to port. He shouted to the helmsman, but there was no time. The ship struck the rocks and ground violently to a halt. The narrows had another victim in its deadly grasp.

He began shouting orders to the crew to assess the damage. The lookout on the port side had been thrown forward, but was not injured. The other two were tossed about, but fortunately neither of them had ended up overboard. Had the ship been moving a few knots faster he may have lost one of them. The port lookout peered over the side, attempting to see if they were taking on water. The captain paced back and forth for what seemed like an eternity. Finally he had the report from below; the hull was intact.

They were aground, but based on the reports, the captain felt confident the *Spokane* could free herself. He dispatched crew throughout the ship to inform the passengers of the situation. Most received the news with relief, including those that had already donned life jackets and were ready to abandon ship. There were a number of injuries, but none appeared to be life-threatening.

The captain had two choices: wait for the next rising tide or attempt to back off the rocks. He dismissed the first idea immediately. To navigate the narrows, you always entered on the rising tide, timing it so you had the maximum water depth to operate in. Waiting through the coming low tide could cause the ship to list and make things worse. No, he had to get off the rocks, and he had to do it now.

* * *

The stewards came through the dining room, tending to the needs of the injured and assuring everyone the ship was not sinking. Things had settled down as passengers were reassured everything was fine.

The bleeding had stopped and even though her head was pounding, Emily was feeling a bit better. John was both scared and proud at the same time. She had not cried at all during the ordeal. A silly thing to think of he thought, and yet it gave him confidence she really could handle this trip into the new and unknown.

"Would you like some tea, miss?" the steward asked.

"Yes, thank you," said Emily.

John opted for a cup of coffee. When the steward returned, John asked about the status of the ship. The steward informed them the ship was intact and the captain was preparing to back off the rocks. While the grounding had been violent, the slow speed of the ship had prevented a breach. The steward also informed them that once they cleared the narrows they would be stopping in Petersburg for inspection.

"Will there be a delay?" said John.

"I'm sorry sir, I don't know," the steward replied as he turned and left.

"Father, do you think we will be delayed?"

"I really don't know Emily. It depends on how much damage there is and whether the captain thinks it's safe to proceed."

"I hope we won't be delayed, I'm anxious enough," said Emily.

"Well, we will just have to be patient and see," her father said with a hint of a smile.

* * *

"Reverse power," the captain ordered, instructing the helmsman to proceed slowly.

The ship shuddered slightly, but remained securely grounded. "Increase power!" shouted the captain. The engine room responded and the ship began to shudder more violently as the propeller churned and beat the water into a froth. Just as the captain was about to abort the effort, the *Spokane* began to move, then just as quickly, stalled.

"All stop," shouted the captain.

The engine room answered and the massive propeller quickly ceased its churning. The *Spokane* had moved several feet and hung up again.

"Shall we try again Captain?" said the helmsman.

"Not yet, we need to see how hard we are hung up before we try again."

The captain ordered another assessment of the hull, both from the forward observers on deck and the crew down below. Within minutes the report came back—she was still sound.

"Let's give it another go," said the captain. "This time we'll apply full reverse immediately and be ready to cut it as soon as we are free."

The last thing the captain wanted was to reverse off the rocks, only to plow the stern aground in the process. The plan was communicated to the engine room and all was ready for the attempt.

"Full reverse now!" ordered the captain.

She shuddered as the boilers delivered full reverse power. Slowly she began to move, groaning as the rocks raked her hull. Within seconds she was free. The crew performed admirably, getting her stopped and forward power applied swiftly to prevent her drifting towards the shore.

The captain breathed a sigh of relief. He quickly called for reports from the bow and the chief engineer to make sure she was still seaworthy. They were in luck; the *Spokane* had survived her encounter with the narrows with just a few bruises and scrapes.

"Ahead slow and keep your eyes out!" the captain ordered.

In the time they were aground the rain had slowed and the wind had eased. *We can make it now*, the captain thought as they proceeded slowly towards Petersburg.

Chapter 11

It had taken another hour, but Thomas had nearly made it to the head of Goat Creek. On the way he had spotted a small grizzly bear high on a ridge. Beyond that, he had seen little else apart from an occasional marmot. There was plenty of moose sign along the trail, but Thomas decided they were probably hunkered down in the middle of the day after feeding in the early morning.

Thomas checked his watch. He had only a short time to spend here before he would need to start back. Returning in the dark through unfamiliar territory wasn't an appealing thought. Thomas pulled the binoculars out of the pack and began surveying the mountains that rimmed the head of the creek. He noted a low pass that lead into the next valley. This was an area he would need to explore next time.

A large glacier occupied a bowl just west of the pass. Thomas had never been close to a glacier. *I should climb up there an get a closer look*, he thought. The idea was short-lived as he realized there was no time for such an impromptu adventure.

There was still snow in the avalanche chutes and higher on the mountains. Thomas continued to scan the hillsides and suddenly they came into view. White dots on the mountain. They were Dall Sheep; twenty or thirty of them just below the snow. They must have just come down through the snow field. Once in the rocks they were easily visible. For a moment, Thomas considered climbing up to see if he could bag one. Quickly he realized they were a lot farther away and a lot higher up than he first thought. *Not enough time today,* he thought. Thomas watched the sheep for a while as they grazed and the spring lambs danced playfully around the group.

Things were looking up, thought Thomas, pleased with how things were going. He had found a promising area to hunt, seen some game, and found no competition from other hunters. It was clear Goat Creek was going to be tough to hunt in a single day. If he was able to find a moose at the lower elevations he could probably do it, but it would make for a very long day. He began making mental note of the additional gear needed for his next trip.

As he finished packing up Thomas noticed the white dots were gone, blended into the snow. He mounted up and headed downstream, daydreaming as the horse meandered along the primitive trail, his thoughts shifting between bags of gold and Emily. The sun was getting low on the horizon by the time he reached the spruce wall. Once they cleared it, the horse moved more quickly, sensing it was time to go home.

Several hours later Thomas arrived at the boarding house, just as the last rays of usable light slipped below the horizon. It had been a good day of exploring and he looked forward to the next trip as soon as he could get outfitted. He took Horse to the barn, took care of the pack and saddle, and worked at brushing her down.

"You did a great job today, old gal," he said as he patted her neck. Horse shook her head up and down and snorted, as if to acknowledge his appreciation.

Just as he finished up, Stella called to him from the porch. "You're late for dinner!" she said sternly. Thomas smiled and thought, *Alright Mother,* and headed to the door.

Chapter 12

The *Spokane* docked briefly in Petersburg while the hull was thoroughly examined. Much of the damage was near waterline and after checking both the exterior and the lower levels of the ship, the captain was satisfied she would make it the rest of the way. Repairs could wait until they reached Seattle. After only an hour or two, the *Spokane* was underway again, making fourteen knots, headed for Juneau.

In his haste to head north from Seattle, John had learned there was no room on any of the ships headed to Valdez. He was able to book passage on the *Spokane* as far as Juneau. From there they would transfer to the *S.S. Northwestern*, one of the vessels operated by the Alaska Steamship Company. Fortunately, passengers departing along the route to Juneau provided a vacancy for John and Emily.

The schedule was tight; they would arrive early on the *Spokane* and depart early evening of the same day on the *Northwestern*. When the ship had ran aground John was worried they might miss their connection, but the delay in Petersburg had been minimal. He had kept his worries to himself, Emily didn't need any further stress.

"You should be more comfortable on the next ship," John said to Emily. "It is a bit bigger than this one."

"I hope so. I am tired of being seasick."

Emily's seasickness had eased once they had reached the Inside Passage and she had been much better since leaving Petersburg. The cut on her forehead had been examined and no stitches were needed. She sported a small bandage and otherwise looked no worse for wear.

"Let's go up on deck and take in some scenery. The air will do you good," said John.

"Father, I'm not sure I want to go on deck."

"Now, now, do as you're told. You'll feel better getting some fresh air and a bit of exercise," said John, shepherding her towards the stairway.

They ventured up on deck and were greeted by one of those magnificent bluebird days in Southeast Alaska. The sun was shining, the seas were calm and the air, while brisk, was refreshing. The *Spokane* slid effortlessly through the sea, with just a hint of spray rising from her bow.

"Look!" exclaimed Emily, pointing excitedly. "Whales!"

John looked and sure enough, a pod of humpback whales were making their way parallel to the ship, a mere one hundred and fifty yards away. The whales slipped silently through the water, moving in concert as their backs broke the surface. Emily was fascinated with the way they moved. As they rounded a small island, John spotted a large group of sea lions basking in the sun. They were sprawled over the rocks just above the water, relaxing and only moving a flipper now and then.

"See, I told you we would see some scenery," said John.

"I have never seen whales or sea lions," Emily said as she leaned over the railing to get a last look at the whales. "This is wonderful."

John was pleased Emily was feeling better and seemed to be enjoying herself. They stayed above deck for a long time, watching the sea birds hover over the ship hoping for some scrap of food. A small group of porpoise were swimming rapidly near the bow of the ship, darting back and forth in the glinting water. This was a world Emily had never imagined. As the sun warmed her face, her thoughts drifted off to Thomas. How she longed to see him and know that he was fine.

"Let's go to the dining room and get some lunch," her

father said, interrupting her daydream. "It's past noon and I'm getting a bit hungry," he said.

Emily realized she was hungry as well, even though she wished she could stay in the sun a while longer.

"I'm ready," she said, smiling at her father. "Let's get something to eat."

* * *

The remainder of the voyage to Juneau was uneventful. Throughout the evening and into the next day, the passengers continued to discuss the grounding and debate the captain's actions, the weather, and everything else even remotely related to the incident. Now they were a mere hour from docking in Juneau.

John resolved not to tell his wife about this part of the trip. She had insisted he send word as soon as they arrived. If he could send a telegram from Valdez she would know immediately, but that of course depended on whether repairs had been completed. Otherwise it would be up to two weeks before his letter reached her.

She had been totally against the trip, trying to talk them out of it till the bitter end. He tried to reassure her they were traveling on excursion ships with first class accommodations. He even brought the brochures from the steamship companies showing young ladies enjoying the sights from the deck of the ship. Of course this made no difference to Lydia. John sometimes wished she could be more supportive and not so stubborn.

"Are you packed?" Emily asked as she entered the state room.

"Almost. But I see you aren't."

"I will race you," she said with a grin.

They finished packing with no clear winner and made sure their bags were tagged properly. The cabin steward would come shortly and take the bags so they would be waiting for them when they went ashore.

"Are you ready to go up topside for the docking?" John asked. Emily nodded and with that, they left the cabin and proceeded to the observation deck.

Most passengers were not departing in Juneau but had booked a round trip excursion taking them all the way to Skagway and then returning to Seattle, stopping in Sitka along the way. John and Emily were among the few leaving the ship when it docked. This gave them several hours to spend in Juneau before the *Northwestern* departed.

As they steamed up the channel, the pounding of stamp mills echoed loudly off the mountains. They were sailing past the largest hardrock gold mines in Alaska. The Treadwell mine on Douglas Island and the Alaska-Juneau Mine produced great amounts of gold from deep underground. It was an impressive sight; the Treadwell Mine to port and the Alaska-Juneau to starboard.

Emily marveled at the size of the facilities. "I thought we were going to the wilderness. These mines are huge, and quite noisy."

"Well, it looks like Alaska is quite civilized. At least this part anyway," said her father, smiling.

"What shall we do in Juneau?"

"First order of business will be to stake out where we will have lunch," he said.

"Always thinking of your stomach, aren't you," she said, smiling slightly.

"And after that, we will walk around a bit and see the sights," said John.

Their plans for the day settled, they both leaned over the rail, hoping to get a view of the town beyond the heads of all the other passengers craning for a glimpse.

* * *

The *Spokane* slipped easily into its mooring at Juneau.
The dock crew scurried around securing the lines and
getting the gang planks in place so the passengers could
depart. Once everything was in place, the unloading of
luggage began and was quickly completed since most
passengers were continuing on the voyage. Satisfied all
was in order, the captain ordered the announcement to
disembark be conveyed throughout the ship. Most chose
to leave the ship and visit the town, especially in light of
the good weather.

John and Emily eventually made their way through
the crowd to the gang plank and departed the ship. John
found their luggage and paid a porter to transfer it to the
holding area for the *Northwestern*. Being reassured it
would be safe there, he and Emily set out to explore the
town of Juneau.

The first thing that struck them was, although it tried
to cater to tourists, it was a mining town at heart. A bit
rough around the edges, there certainly was none of the
high society airs Emily experienced in Seattle. She was
fascinated by the town and its people. It was a busy place,
ships unloading cargo, fishing boats coming and going
from the small harbor, and men busy moving goods to
the mines. She began to get the sense of adventure that
had compelled Thomas to go north.

Time passed quickly as they viewed the town, walking up and down the narrow streets lined with small shops
and houses. Before they knew it, lunch time had arrived;
they turned in to a little eatery and sat down. A waitress
walked up to the table, paused, and gave them the once
over.

"You new in town?" she asked as she plopped the menu down.

"We are here just for the day," said John. "Catching the Northwestern this afternoon and heading north."

"The Northwestern eh?" she said knowingly. "You know about that ship right?"

"About all we know is it is going to Valdez and we were able to get passage on it. Why? Is there something wrong with it?" John asked.

"No, there's nothing wrong with it—unless you consider running aground every trip or two normal," the waitress said flatly.

"Well, we certainly haven't heard about that," said John.

"Ask anybody," she said. "Now, what can I get you?"

"What's good?" asked John.

"Well, let's see. We have some fresh King Salmon and two day old stew. Take your pick."

"We'll take the salmon. Sound good to you Emily?"

"Yes, let's try it."

The waitress took their order and retreated without saying anything further. Little did John and Emily know the *Northwestern* had quite a reputation. In fact, it held the record for the most groundings in Alaska than any other ship. Some also said she had nine lives, because few of the incidents had resulted in any significant damage. The *Northwestern* seemed to have taken a particular liking to Eagle Beach just north of Juneau. She was seen grounded there on the mud at low tide enough times to be an embarrassment to the steamship company.

"I'm scared, Father," Emily said with a worried look on her face. "That ship doesn't sound safe at all!"

"I'm sure it will be fine Emily. The waitress was

probably exaggerating."

"I hope so. After being sick so much of the time on the first ship, I don't want to have any more trouble."

Within a few minutes, the waitress returned with their food and placed it unceremoniously in front of them. "Enjoy," she said as she walked away.

Emily looked down at her plate. The large chunk of fried salmon sat next to a fist-sized glob of white rice, along with something that looked like it might have been a vegetable at some point in time.

"Looks wonderful," said Emily, frowning.

"Better than nothing I guess," said John.

Picking through their food, they looked out the window with a clear view down the channel they had traveled on their way into Juneau. In the distance was a large plume of black smoke, billowing from a steamer.

"That might be our ship," said John. "If so, it's running way ahead of schedule."

They continued watching as the ship slowly made its way past the mines toward the docks.

"Excuse me miss," John said as the waitress passed by. "Is that the Northwestern coming in?"

The waitress paused and looked out the window. "Yup, that's it."

"You finished?" she asked. John and Emily both nodded and she cleared their half empty plates away. "Anything else?"

"No, that will be all, thank you," said John.

She reached into the pocket of her apron and slapped the check onto the table. From his wallet, John handed her enough to cover the bill plus a modest tip. She took the money, and, giving them one last look said, "Good luck with the ship." Before John could reply, she turned and walked away.

"My, she was rather rude," said Emily.

"She certainly is short with people. Come on, let's go down and watch the ship come in."

Leaving the eatery they headed to greet the ship. The *Northwestern* was almost close enough to tie up when they reached the dock. She was bigger than the *Spokane*, a fact that should have inspired confidence in them, but the waitress had destroyed any such hope. The lines were thrown ashore and the dock crew quickly made them secure and drew the ship in slowly to the bumpers. The engine noise decreased and the crew made fast the gang planks to prepare for disembarkation.

John looked up at the ship. She looked sound and sturdy, being longer and heavier than the *Spokane*. It wasn't as new as the *Spokane*, but John had been assured when he booked passage in Seattle she was a fine and luxurious ship. After talking with the waitress he had some doubts. He would inquire about her reputation before they boarded.

Chapter 13

"How was your scouting trip?" Stella asked as she brought dinner in from the kitchen.

Thomas sat down as Stella slid a plate piled high with fried potatoes and a nice chunk of moose steak in front of him. Thomas eagerly dug in to his meal, realizing how hungry he was after his adventure.

"Well?" she said.

Thomas gulped down the bite. "It was great. I found a way into Goat Creek"

"Really? That's interesting since most people have given up on that valley."

"Actually, I didn't find the way, Horse did," Thomas admitted. "I think she's been up there before by the way she acted. Did Wesley ever hunt up there?"

Stella thought for a moment and said, "He hunted all over this country, but he never really told me the details. It always worried me because I never knew where to look for him if he didn't come home."

"Well I'm betting he did, because your old horse seemed to know just how to get up there."

"Did you see any critters?" she asked as she returned from the kitchen with her own dinner.

"I saw a bear up high on the ridge and a lot of sheep way up at the head of the valley. But it's not going to be easy hunting there without spending a night or two," Thomas said between bites.

"I understand," said Stella. "Wesley used to be gone days at a time."

"I'm going to need a tent and some other camping gear in order to do it right," said Thomas, hoping silently that Stella had some stashed away somewhere.

"I have a spare coffee pot and things you'll need to cook with, but Wesley had everything else with him the last time he went out. I guess we could get you some down at Noel's place," she said.

Thomas didn't want to impose on her any more than he already had. He hated not paying his own way and was indebted to her too much already.

"No, I'll work out a way to do some day hunts until we get a bit of money coming in, then we'll think about outfitting me right."

"Are you sure you can get by doing it that way?" she asked.

"I saw plenty of moose sign lower in the valley. I think if I work it right I can bag one and get out of there before dark, but I'll have to leave real early," he said.

"Well if you wait another month or so we'll have nearly eighteen hours of daylight," she said, smiling.

Thomas hadn't thought of that. The days were getting longer and, even though he had heard about the perpetual daylight in the north, he had to experience it.

"I'm going to head back up there early tomorrow and see what I can do," he said.

"Okay, I'll make you a good lunch, but I want you to be careful with the bears up there," said Stella.

"I'm not worried about the bears," said Thomas, grinning. "I've got some good medicine for them if they get to nosey."

"Don't get too cocky young man," said Stella, wagging her finger at him. "You are still a greenhorn you know," she said, smiling ever so slightly.

"I know, but I'm working on it," he said, returning the smile.

Thomas finished up his dinner and decided to make

it an early night. He needed the rest; after all, tomorrow was going to be a long and productive day—at least he hoped it would turn out that way.

* * *

He woke up later than he planned. The long day before had taken its toll and he had to drag himself out of bed. Thomas had planned to sneak out early but already he could hear Stella scurrying around in the kitchen. He realized it was probably the smell of coffee brewing that woke him. He got dressed quickly, mildly agitated that he already was off to a slow start.

"How come you didn't wake me?" Thomas asked as he shuffled into the kitchen.

Stella had her back to him, cooking up something on the big iron stove. Without turning around she said, "I didn't know what time you wanted to leave so I was going to wake you when I was done cooking. Since you're up, run out and get me some more wood for the stove so I can finish up your breakfast."

Thomas pulled on his coat and went out the back door, headed for the woodshed. As he stepped outside, the crisp morning air struck him, almost stinging his face. Already it was beginning to get light outside, making him feel all the more anxious to get the day started. He grabbed up as much wood as he could cradle in his arms and returned to the kitchen.

"Here you go," he said as he dropped the wood into the box next to the stove. "I really wanted to get going early today."

"Your breakfast is almost ready. Get a cup of coffee and sit down," she said as she busily finished frying up the potatoes and putting the final touch on the sausage.

Thomas grabbed his favorite cup, poured some coffee and plopped down at the dining room table. A minute later, Stella brought his plate and sat down across from him with a cup of tea.

"I'm sorry you didn't get going sooner, but this is better anyway. You won't have to stumble around in the dark."

"I know, but I also don't want to be coming back in the dark either," he said. "I'll just have to make sure I don't shoot anything too late in the day."

Thomas ate quickly while Stella gave him a look that made him realize he was acting a bit like a hungry dog. He apologized as he got up and left to get the rifle and other things from his room.

As he breezed back through the dining room headed for the back door, Stella handed him his lunch. He grabbed it without slowing down. "Thanks," he said as he opened the back door.

"Be careful," Stella shouted as the door slammed behind him. "And be back before dark!"

* * *

Thomas worked quickly to saddle up the horse and get his gear secured. The horse sensed his urgency, but didn't share it. Thomas led Horse out, mounted up, and headed off to Goat Creek.

His plan had been to get there early and hunt the lower valley, hoping to find a moose, field dress it, and get home before sundown. He knew the moose bedded down in the middle of the day, coming out occasionally when they needed a drink. Being late would make his job harder.

He reached the river without incident and let Horse take the lead to the spruce wall. He tried not to be in too much of a hurry, knowing full well it was possible to find a moose anywhere along the way. At the spruce wall, Horse hesitated, apparently not thrilled to make the climb two days in a row. Thomas gently urged her along and they continued through and on up the trail.

An hour later they had reached an area near a small lake where the horse had access to grass and Thomas could use the binoculars to glass the hills for game. It was a clear day, not hot, but the weather was pleasant. He tied up the horse, realizing if a bear came along while he was gone he would be walking home. Knowing Wesley, the horse had likely been trained to stay put during a hunt, but they weren't that good of friends yet.

Thomas grabbed his binoculars and pack and took the rifle for a short walk up to a small ridge that paralleled the valley. At the top of the ridge he had a good view of a draw that went up the mountain on the east side of the valley.

He picked out a dry spot and sat down in the warming sun to glass. An hour passed, then two. He continued to glass the alder patches and willow thickets looking for a moose he hoped was there. Thinking of moving on, he was about to head back down the ridge when he saw it.

Chapter 14

The passengers streamed down the gang planks of the *Northwestern*, talking excitedly, many relieved to be on solid ground for at least a few hours. It was too early for John and Emily to board the ship; besides they needed to ensure the transfer of their luggage was in order and John definitely wanted to inquire about the ship's misadventures.

They found the small building that housed the steamship company's offices and ticketing agent. Since the ship had arrived early there were few people waiting in line to talk to the agent. Most people had booked passage all the way through from Seattle; there were only a handful of new passengers that would board at Juneau.

When they reached the head of the line, the ticket agent asked, "How may I help you sir?"

John explained to him they had arrived on the *Spokane* earlier and he wanted to ensure their luggage was scheduled for transfer to the *Northwestern*.

"Your name sir?" asked the agent.

"John Palmer."

"Just a moment sir," said the agent as he began shuffling paper and looking through the manifest. "Ah, here it is," he said. "Yes, your luggage has been queued up and is ready to be loaded when the time comes. May I see your tickets please?"

John handed the agent their tickets and he quickly checked off their names.

"Everything is in order sir. I'm afraid we won't be boarding for a couple of hours. They are busy cleaning staterooms and restocking some supplies. Would you like a map and timetable?

"Yes, thank you," said John, taking the page-sized map from the agent.

Is there anything else, sir?"

"I have heard this ship seems to have had a number of accidents. Is this true?" asked John.

The agent looked down, shuffled from one foot to the other, and said "She's a fine ship sir."

"I can see that. But what about these rumors we heard about her running aground all the time?"

"She's a fine ship sir. There were a few minor little things in the past but our captain and crew are the best there is," the agent said, minimizing the truth. "Don't worry sir, you won't have any trouble."

His response did little to reassure them. During the conversation, Emily's face grew progressively worried. The voyage on the *Spokane* had been tough on her with the seasickness and then the grounding in the narrows. While she left the details to her father, she knew this stage of the voyage would cross the Gulf of Alaska, a substantial stretch of unprotected waters. She was not looking forward to it in the first place and now even less so.

The agent validated their tickets, informed them boarding time would be in about two hours, and said the ship would blast the horn three times when boarding was available.

With that, they left the ticket office and walked along the dock, surveying the ship. According to the brochure John picked up in Seattle, she was built in 1889 in Pennsylvania, originally working the route between New York and Havana, Cuba. At nearly three-hundred feet long and 3,500 tons she was a substantial ship. She looked to be in good repair and well kept. John wondered if the rumors were just that and nothing more.

"Father, I'm nervous about this voyage," said Emily as she peered over the dock at the bow of the ship. "Do you think it is safe?"

"I think we will be fine. It looks to be a sturdy ship and the agent said the captain and crew are the finest," John said, trying to convince himself as much as he was Emily.

"Will the seas be rough?" she asked, knowing the ship would be fully exposed to the potential fury of the Pacific.

"It depends on the weather and we have no way of knowing," replied John.

Looking at the map, John examined the voyage ahead. The route would take them south from Juneau, around the tip of Douglas Island, then north through Lynn Canal to Skagway. After a stop there, the ship would turn south back down Lynn Canal then west through Icy Strait and Cross Sound.

Once they exited the sound they would be in the Gulf, exposed to anything the Pacific chose to throw at them. The trip across the open water would take at least a day, maybe longer depending on the weather.

Waiting for departure, John and Emily returned to walking along the narrow streets of Juneau. Juneau was an old town as far as Alaska towns went, being established as a small camp in 1880. Now it was a bustling mining town driven by the lust for hardrock gold. There were small shops offering a variety of goods. John and Emily couldn't help but think how different this was than Seattle. They were a long way from home and the journey was only half over.

Anxious to continue their journey, John and Emily made their way back to the dock early. By the time the ship horn sounded three times, they were standing at the gangplank ready to board.

*　*　*

Smoke belched from the stack as the *Northwestern* eased away from the dock and made the slow turn towards the south. John and Emily had already been to their cabin and unpacked, returning topside in time to watch the ship depart. There were no waving crowds or well-wishers on the dock like in Seattle; only workmen stowing luggage carts and mooring ropes. The *Northwestern* shuddered as she completed her turn and the captain ordered full ahead. As she steamed down Gastineau Channel, the sun began to set. The lights of the Treadwell mine complex burned brightly as they steamed past. The sea was calm and the air crisp, an evening to be enjoyed.

John and Emily watched as the lights of Juneau and then Treadwell slipped away, leaving them surrounded by the clear Alaska night illuminated by a full moon. The *Northwestern* was now making fifteen knots, steaming towards the turn around the southern tip of Douglas Island.

"Are you hungry yet?" said John.

"A little," she said.

"Let's go to the dining room and see if we can get some dinner."

They left the deck and made their way to the dining room. It wasn't crowded, but there were a number of passengers seated about, enjoying their meal.

"Where are we now?" asked Emily, pointing at the large map of the route that covered the wall near the entrance to the dining room.

John looked at the map and quickly found their location, or at least what he thought was close to where they were.

"I think we are here," he said pointing at the map. "Nearly to the end of Douglas Island. We should start to turn right again and go north."

John traced the route north and realized they soon would be passing Eagle Beach, a vast muddy stretch of beach formed by the glacially fed river. Since it reached far out into Lynn Canal, it became a hazard at low tide for seafarers that weren't attentive to their course. *Sometimes it's better not to know*, John thought to himself.

They found a seat in the dining room and the waiter efficiently provided them with a menu.

"What are you going to have Emily?" asked her father.

"I think I will eat something light in case I get sick again."

"Me too," said John, "Even though I haven't been sick—yet."

The waiter returned and they both ordered the fresh caught King salmon that had been procured in Juneau, with a side of steamed potatoes. While they were waiting, the conversation turned once again to the voyage ahead.

"Do you think we will be safe on this ship?" Emily asked her father.

As John pondered how to answer, a voice from behind them said "Excuse me, I couldn't help but overhear your question. May I join you?"

Emily and John both turned to look at the man seated alone behind them. He was probably in his late fifties, gray hair down to his shoulders and a beard that extended to the middle of his chest. His face was brown and leathery with abundant wrinkles. Despite his appearance, he seemed to have a pleasant demeanor. Emily thought he looked like Santa Claus.

John immediately stood and extended his hand.

"Of course sir. Please join us. My name is John Palmer and this is my daughter Emily."

"Thank you sir, I'm Ezekiel Shaw. Pleased to meet you both," he said as he pulled up a chair.

"So Mister Shaw, is this your first voyage north?" asked John.

Shaw chuckled a bit and replied, "No, I've been up and down this coast more times than I can count. And please, my friends call me Zeke."

"Alright then Zeke, where are you headed?" John asked.

"I'm headed to the Porucupine District outside of Haines to see if I can find some work on one of the placer claims."

"Oh, you're a miner then," said John.

"Yep, been doing it for nigh on twenty-five years now."

"Have you struck it rich?" asked Emily.

Zeke laughed. "Young lady, if I had struck it rich do you think I would be on this scow headed north?"

Emily blushed at his response.

"I'm sorry little lady, I didn't mean no disrespect. It's just I get asked that all the time," said Zeke. "I've worked the underground mines and the placers. Never been able to strike it on my own so I end up working for someone else."

"You called this ship a scow. Any particular reason?" asked John.

"Nothing other than my cynical attitude I guess," said Zeke. "But I heard the young lady ask if it was safe so I thought I would join you and toss in my two cents."

With that, Zeke began to tell John and Emily about all the groundings, strandings, and sinkings that had taken place throughout Alaska in the last twenty-five years.

"Then there was the *Nellie Martin* that ran aground just about in this spot right here. But the worst was the *Islander*. That was a bad one."

Zeke explained the *Islander* had left Skagway loaded with miners from the Klondike bringing their fortunes south after a successful summer in 1901. About twelve miles south of Juneau she hit something, an iceberg or rock and sank.

"Over sixty souls were lost in that one. And tons of gold, straight to the bottom," said Zeke.

John looked at Emily to see her reaction. Her head was down and she was picking at her food. He could see she was uneasy.

"Surely this ship is safe though," said John.

"Well she's had her fair share of trouble, but nothing major. I remember being hung up on Eagle Beach waiting for the tide a year or so back," said Zeke. "Plenty of opportunity for trouble coming up between here and Skagway. You got Eagle Reef, Vanderbilt Reef, and Eldred Rock ahead. Everyone of them has scored their fair share of ships in the past."

John thought maybe changing the subject would help Emily get her mind off shipwrecks and seasickness.

"Emily and I are headed for Valdez. Have you ever been there?"

"Valdez, eh? Never been there. I'm not too excited about crossing the Gulf in one of these steamers," said Zeke. "Look at what happened to the *Bessie Reuter* and the *Annie*. Both lost with all hands in the Gulf. Nope, not for me."

Well that didn't help, thought John.

"And then there was that schooner, what was it named?

Oh, the *Lincoln*. She hit hurricane winds in the Gulf and went missing," said Zeke.

John looked at Emily and could see she was getting paler by the moment.

"Well, Mr. Shaw, I can see Emily is not feeling well so I believe it is time for us to return to our cabin."

"I hope I didn't scare you little lady. Was just stating some facts. I'll bet my last dollar you'll get to Valdez in fine shape," said Zeke, laughing loudly.

From the look on her face, his attempt to make amends had little effect.

John and Emily stood, said goodnight to Shaw and left the dining room.

Hmmph. Cheechakos, Zeke thought as he took Emily's plate and began to scavenge.

Chapter 15

Thomas was lost. The moose went down with the first shot, at least he thought it did, but when Thomas broke through the alders it was gone. Tracking the blood trail through the thick brush for several hours with his head down to the ground had left him confused and weary. Now he had no idea which way to turn.

Thomas searched in vain for the blood trail, his hopes of recovering the moose all but gone. Daylight was fading and with it the temperatures had begun to drop. Faced with a night in the wilderness with little provision, he began to make his way out of the thick alders to a more suitable location for camp.

The setting sun backlit the mountains. The last traces of light cast their rays from behind the peaks, leaving the valley gray. Shadows took on vague shapes; everything faded into a wash of drab colors. Thomas had dropped his pack right before pulling the trigger. Now he regretted his carelessness; he had no provisions and no shelter. He thought about trying to retrace his steps but in the growing darkness it would be futile—and dangerous.

At least I have tobacco and matches, Thomas thought to himself. Not that he wanted a cigarette, but with dry wood he could at least have a fire to give some heat and light. Making his way out of the alders he climbed to a small knoll dotted with spruce trees. Though not the largest of trees, they offered some shelter under the dense boughs.

Thomas propped the .45-70 up against a small spruce and set about foraging for wood. He was angry with himself; angry for fouling the shot, losing the moose, and most of all for getting lost without any of his gear.

With no axe or saw, Thomas resigned himself to breaking off the biggest of the dead branches in hopes of collecting enough for the night. The dead branches from the spruce trees were good and dry and they burned well—too well to provide heat for any length of time. As the sun finally vanished, the cold of the Alaska night settled into the valley. Though it was late spring, temperatures at this elevation still dipped below freezing at night. Thomas shivered as he thought about all the snow still capping the mountains and filling many of the little draws and valleys. The remnants of winter held strong; it was going to be cold.

The fire easily crackled to life, the dry spruce burning in earnest as if Thomas had doused it with kerosene. With the branches stacked high, Thomas settled in for the night. Leaning up against a large spruce he pulled his coat tight around him, stuffed his hands under his arms and tried to get some sleep; it was going to be a long day tomorrow.

He awoke with a start, unsure of where he was for a moment. The fire had died down to a few glowing embers and the darkness was now full. Suddenly he heard it; a twig snap somewhere behind him. Thomas immediately reached down at his side for the .45-70 and grabbed a handful of moss. Frantically he searched around with his hands, finding only the soft, damp moss and spruce needles. The thought came slowly to him, *The gun's against a tree somewhere.* Now in the darkness he had no idea where it was. Another twig snap, then two. The noise was closer this time.

Thomas rolled slowly to his knees and sweeping his arms around found what was left of his spruce branches. He scooped up as many has he could and placed them on the embers. Nothing happened. Taking his hat he fanned the embers rapidly, hoping to ignite the jumble of branches. Still the fire refused to cooperate. Thomas didn't want to make a bunch of noise. Quietly he smashed the branches down into the embers and fanned them again. The spruce exploded into flames, jumping high into the air. In the dancing glow of the flames Thomas could see the .45-70 ten feet away, leaning against the tree where he had left it.

While the fire illuminated the immediate area, it was a bit like looking into the sun; Thomas couldn't see much beyond it. As the fire crackled and smoked, Thomas listened intently, straining to hear the noise that had set him on edge. Nothing. *The fire must've scared it away.* But still, having the cold steel of the rifle in hand would give him more comfort.

Thomas started to crawl quietly towards the gun, stopping to look around every few feet. Most would have probably yelled and screamed to make themselves known; Thomas on the other hand, thought it would be giving away his position. And he felt foolish yelling and screaming if it turned out to be a porcupine or a rabbit—despite the fact there was no one around for miles to hear him yell.

A few more feet and the gun would be his. He stopped and looked up, first towards the gun, then back towards the fire—then he saw it. No, he saw *them.* Spirit-like shadows moving just beyond the fire. He stared to see what they were but the more he tried to look past the fire, the less he could see. There was nothing to do but get the gun. Thomas lunged the last few feet, grabbed the .45-70 and rolled to a sitting position, his back against the small spruce. He hadn't reloaded after the shot at the moose; racking the lever action he pointed past the fire and pulled the trigger only to be rewarded with a sickening click as the firing pin struck empty space. The gun was empty. *Amateur!* he thought as he fumbled in his pocket for cartridges.

As Thomas searched his pockets for the shells, the shadows continuing to move slowly just beyond the fire, time slowed down. The panic left him; his mind began to clear. He realized shooting blindly was a waste of what little ammunition he had. He had to be smart. Thrusting his hand into the only pocket left he found the cartridges and quickly loaded the gun and worked the lever—now he was ready.

The shadows moved closer and the flames shone in their eyes—wolves. There were four of them; a small pack. Thomas was shocked they would come this close, stalking a human sitting next to a fire. He was worried about his back. They were pack hunters and had mastered the art and tactics of the stalk. He couldn't get them all; the rest of his ammunition was in his pack, lost somewhere in the dark. He had three cartridges and had to make the most of them.

Thomas yelled at the wolves. They remained. *Some stand-off*, he thought. He really hated to use what ammunition he had left, after all he had a long hike left to even find his pack and this was bear country—big grizzly country.

Suddenly the large wolf on the left lunged past the fire straight at Thomas. The .45-70 came up and barked once, rolling the wolf over backwards and killing it instantly, just as the second wolf rounded the fire on his right. Thomas worked the lever and swung the rifle in one smooth action and dropped the second wolf in its tracks. Two down, two left, one cartridge. *This is not good.*

The remaining wolves were prowling back and forth, staying just out of sight beyond the fire. Thomas shifted his position a bit to get a better look but could see nothing. The moments passed slowly as the fire burned down, making it a little easier to see beyond it. For what seemed like an eternity Thomas strained his eyes to locate the remaining wolves. They were gone; the silence had returned. It was then Thomas began to shake, the adrenaline surge overtaking his body. He quickly threw as many branches as he could grab on the fire and crawled slowly back to the large spruce, the .45-70 clutched firmly in his right hand. There would be no sleep tonight.

* * *

In the morning, Thomas skinned the wolves. The first was a large male, probably more than 140 pounds. The second was a smaller female but still a large wolf. Both had excellent pelts; even though it was spring they hadn't begun to shed. Though he didn't relish the thought of packing two green wolf hides out with him, they would bring a few dollars from the fur trader back in town—and he needed the money.

He was hungry, very hungry, and yet he couldn't bring himself to eat wolf meat. The fire was out anyway and he was tired of the whole the situation—he would eat when he found his pack.

It took him a while, but Thomas made a crude pack frame from alder branches lashed together with spruce root. He tied the green pelts to the frame and was able to hoist it on his back, and while it was uncomfortable, it worked.

In the daylight, Thomas could see the valley below where he had spent hours the day before busting brush in search of the moose. The small knoll where he spent the night was part of a low ridge that paralleled the valley but was sparsely populated with spruce and waist-high brush. This would be easier walking than the alder pit below. He began working his way down the ridge line in the direction he had come from the day before.

His last round was in the chamber, ready for action. He only hoped he wouldn't need it and if he did, he hoped one would be enough.

* * *

By mid-morning Thomas reached the end of the ridge. The easy walking was over; the thick tangle of alders awaited him. He slipped off the crude pack and sat down on the hillside to survey what lay ahead. The valley was wide with a stream that wound its way through the alder thickets. Here and there were areas of swampy ground that were near impossible to negotiate. Thomas rolled a cigarette and took his time smoking. He was very hungry and thinking constantly of the meager rations waiting in his pack.

There was no easy way out; he would have to bust brush again, but at least from up here he could plan somewhat of a route. He finished his cigarette and smashed it into the ground then took one last look around. And then he saw it. Just a small patch of brown at first, then the flick of an ear, the turn of a head. It was a moose, probably his moose judging from its size. He couldn't be sure of course, but if it was he had to finish the job. The moose was laying on the edge of a clearing, mostly concealed by the alders.

From his vantage point Thomas could see further down the valley, all the way to the small lake near where he first saw the moose. Now he had his bearings. He only hoped his pack horse was still there on the far side of the lake and hadn't fallen prey to the wolves or a bear.

It was clear now the moose had veered off the day before and circled back towards the lake. Thomas had lost the blood trail and instead of turning, had continued on up the valley away from the moose. The wind was in his favor, blowing up the valley. Thomas planned to drop down near the stream and slowly work his way toward the moose.

After nearly an hour he was in position. It was the same moose; he could see it was wounded and suffering. He sighed heavily, resolving never to miss a shot again. Easing quietly up to a fallen tree, he rested the rifle across it. He was shaking inside but wasn't sure why. This wasn't the first animal he had shot, but somehow it was different.

He took a long, deep breath and let it out slowly, hoping to calm his nerves. Thomas took aim just behind the ear, drew another deep breath, let half of it out, and held it. He squeezed the trigger slowly until the .45-70 let loose. The moose flinched slightly, it's head dropping to the ground, antlers twisting to one side as life drained away.

Thomas had never seen a moose close up. As he approached he quickly realized two things: it was larger than the whitetails back home and this was not going to be an easy job. It was a bull, however the antlers were small since they had just started to regrow after being shed last fall.

There was really no difference in how you field dressed an animal, it was just a matter of size. The first problem was getting the moose rolled over. Since Thomas shot it while it was laying down, it collapsed in a kneeling position. Thomas grabbed the antlers and pulled, trying to roll the moose on it's side. It didn't budge. It became clear he had to get the legs out from under it in order to roll it over.

After a few minutes of tugging and pulling he was able to get the front legs out to one side. This time pulling on the antlers moved the moose half way over, the hind legs now preventing it from going all the way. At least he could get to the hind legs now. With much effort he pulled the closest one out. One final pull on the antlers flopped the moose onto its side. Thomas was nearly worn out, breathing hard with beads of sweat on his forehead—and he hadn't even gotten started.

Without any rope, he had to whittle off some small poles to prop the legs up and apart in order to open the moose and gut it. It was a shaky system and Thomas had to repeatedly reposition the legs in order to get the job done. It was a messy affair and by the time he had quartered the moose he was pretty much covered in blood and hair. His knife had began to dull but he had no recourse since the sharpening stone was back in his pack. With the quarters off and resting on some spruce boughs he whittled from a nearby tree, Thomas decided to leave the ribs attached until he returned with the horse and his axe.

He marked the spot by tying his bright red handkerchief to the tallest tree he could bend over, then letting it spring back high into the air. Confident the location was adequately marked, Thomas headed for the lake to first fetch his pack, then find Horse.

It was a long walk, but only because he was so tired and hungry. He had thought about cooking up some moose meat right at the kill site, but in the interest of time, decided against it.

The pack was where he had left it, undisturbed by any of the four-footed locals. Nearly shaking, he ate ravenously, mixing mouthfuls of jerky with big bites of bread Stella had packed for him, washing it all down with water from his canteen. Feeling a bit refreshed, he headed around the lake and, to his delight, there was the horse, right where he left her. While tied up with a length of rope she had plenty of grass to feed on, but no water. Thomas planned to be gone an hour rather than overnight. He untied the horse and led her the short distance to the lake where she drank for a long time.

It didn't take long to find his way to the downed moose. Thomas was able to ride most of the way, only leading the horse around some of the deeper, swampy areas. At the kill site, Thomas worked quickly to construct a travois, a pole sled, to transport the meat. Without it he would be walking back to town. There was no way the horse could carry a whole moose and him at the same time.

Using his axe, he cut two long spruce poles as the main supports, then lashed enough cross poles to allow him to secure the quarters of the moose. He removed the ribs from the moose using the axe and his knife.

Thomas stood, placed both hands on his hips and stretched backwards as far as he could, then bent forward and touched the ground. His hands were cramping and his back was stiff. *This job can't be done soon enough,* he thought.

He looked at the antlers and guessed they were no more than twenty-five inches wide. He debated on whether to take them, ultimately deciding not to—it wasn't much of a trophy; he had enough to deal with.

After the events of the last twenty-four hours, the quarters seemed incredibly heavy as he struggled to load them on the travois.

Three hours after the shot, the moose was loaded up and Thomas was trudging along, leading the horse through the brush towards the trail that would take them to town. His first hunt wasn't what he had imagined it would be, but it was a success. Thomas had received his first schooling from the wilds of Alaska.

He thought of Wesley.

Chapter 16

As they slept, the *Northwestern* silently steamed by the hazards of Lynn Canal. By the time John and Emily woke, Skagway was in sight. They went up to the observation deck and watched as the ship slowed and carefully slipped towards the dock. Despite their worries, the whole journey from Juneau was uneventful.

"See Emily, I told you we would be fine," said John, thankful they had made it past most of Shaw's horror stories from the night before. Emily was looking much refreshed as they descended to the dining room for some breakfast.

As John sipped his morning coffee, he looked at the timetable. Their stay in Skagway would be fairly short while cargo was offloaded and supplies restocked for the next leg of the voyage across the Gulf to Cordova. If all went well, in three days time they would be in Valdez.

That was the good news. The bad news was, once they exited Cross Sound into the Gulf, four-hundred miles of open ocean lie between them and the protection of the islands of Prince William Sound. With good seas and no wind, the *Northwestern* could make eighteen knots. This meant nearly twenty-four hours exposed to the open ocean. Their journey had been tough so far, but the most dangerous part still lay ahead.

John and Emily chose not to go ashore, instead enjoying a leisurely breakfast while looking out the windows at the scenery of Skagway. Emily had carefully looked around the dining room when they first entered, hoping not to see Ezekiel Shaw. She didn't care much for his stories and didn't want to be reminded of the hazards of ocean travel.

Emily recalled from their conversation that he was

headed to Haines. Since father told her the *Northwestern* didn't stop there, he must have left the ship already to catch another that would take him the short distance to his destination.

"I really didn't like that man," she said, staring out the window.

"Mr. Shaw? I know he made you nervous with his stories. But look, here we are safe and sound in Skagway."

"I can't wait to get to Valdez," she said. "And I really can't wait to see Thomas!"

"Another three days and we should be there. I hope we don't have any trouble finding him," said John.

"How long before we leave here?"

"I think we have just a few hours," said John, referring to the timetable. "Let's try and relax and before you know it, we'll be on our way."

Four hours later the *Northwestern* pulled away from the dock, turned south, and steamed steadily down Lynn Canal towards Icy Strait.

* * *

The ship pitched violently as the sixty-knot winds struck her broadside. Since leaving Cross Sound, the weather had deteriorated with each passing mile. The seas were rocking the ship and the wind from the south threatened to drive her ashore. The captain had ordered all passengers to their cabins and secured the ship. They were still making progress, but had slowed to minimize the strain on the ship.

It had taken nearly nine hours from Skagway to reach Cross Sound and enter the Gulf. Nightfall was upon them, making the storm seem all the worse. As the winds increased in intensity, the captain weighed his options. He could attempt to find shelter in a bay or ride it out and hope the storm didn't get any worse. The next gust of wind convinced him of the need to wait it out. He pulled out the chart, looking for shelter.

The captain was no rookie. He knew the options for refuge were few and far between along this stretch of coast. He calculated their position at thirty-five miles northwest of Cross Sound, making twelve knots. This put them fifteen miles from the nearest shelter at Lituya Bay. It would take over an hour of being pounded by the wind and waves to reach the bay, but he had no choice. Turning around wasn't an option. He just hoped they could navigate with the full moon and make it to shelter before the storm worsened.

* * *

Emily was laying across the bed, sobbing uncontrollably. With each gust of wind the ship shuddered and rumbled, intensifying her anguish. She had been sick for the last two hours. John could do nothing. So far he had fought back the sickness, but being in the cabin, the pounding of the waves was making it difficult even for him. He tried to comfort Emily but in reality knew it would do no good. The only thing that would help was to end the storm and that wasn't within his power.

"I know we're going to die out here and Thomas will never know what happened to me!"

John knew his daughter was at times melodramatic but this wasn't one of them. She was genuinely afraid and to be truthful, so was he. So far they had no word from the captain after the initial order to return to their cabins. He wished he could find out what was happening, but dared not leave the cabin. He turned his attention to Emily, trying in vain to comfort her.

"We'll be fine Emily. I'm sure this storm will be over very soon," said John, knowing she would no doubt see through the lie.

"Why does it have to be so hard? All I wanted was to be with Thomas," she said, tears streaming down her face.

"We knew before we started it might be a difficult trip. But I guess neither of us realized how bad it could be," said John.

"But it is getting worse all the time!"

"Just hold on a little longer dear and we will be fine."

John all but gave up trying to comfort her. They just had to ride it out and hope for the best. It was out of their hands. He prayed the ship would hold together and the captain would make the right choices.

* * *

Entering Lituya Bay was tricky. It was narrow and elongated, stretching perpendicular to the coast. With the wind coming from the southwest, the waves would pile into the entrance. Adding to that, when the tide was running there was a five knot current that had to be dealt with. Worst case would be coming in with a sixty knot wind to your back in a following sea, riding a five knot current.

It's like rushing headlong into the abyss, thought the captain, but this was the hand he had been dealt. The wind had not relented and the waves were cresting at eight feet now. It was going to be tricky.

Inside the bay was a small, circular island roughly two miles from the entrance. Behind it they could anchor and be out of the wind and worst of the waves.

With the entrance to the bay in view, the captain informed the helm and crew of the plan. They were on a rising tide, which meant the current would be flowing strong into the bay. Once they made the turn to starboard the wind and waves would be at their back, further complicating navigation. To compensate, when they were along side the entrance to the bay the helm would turn hard to starboard and increase the engines to full. It was the only way to maintain control of the ship. None of the crew were particularly happy with this plan but knowing they had little choice, they were ready to comply.

The entrance loomed before them as the *Northwestern* turned and increased to full power. The captain prayed the engines wouldn't fail him now. As they neared the entrance, the effect of the incoming current could be felt at the helm. The ship became slow to respond and sluggish, the bow wandering back and forth from its intended course.

The captain estimated a half mile or so of bad current before they were far enough into the bay to be free of its effect. The helmsman worked feverishly to keep the ship on course. They successfully passed the point to the west of the entrance and the bay ever so slowly began to widen ahead of them.

The sea would not let go of them so easily, however, sending one last gust that must have topped hurricane force. The bow swung suddenly to starboard, pointing them directly at the rocks of the entrance. The helmsman spun the wheel frantically to port while the captain swore and wished he had more power. The ship slowly began to turn from the rocks. Everyone on the bridge held their breath until she came about, narrowly escaping disaster.

After what seemed like an eternity, the sea relented; they had made it into Lituya Bay. Briefly the captain considered waiting out the storm in Anchorage Cove located to the west, just inside the bay. He dismissed the idea; the low spit separating the cove from the Gulf wouldn't provide enough protection. The ship would roll and pitch all night, giving the passengers little opportunity for rest. They would press on.

Once out of the current, the captain ordered the helmsman to hug the eastern shore of the bay, as this provided more protection. The wind from the Gulf was still blowing fiercely and the waves substantial, but the further they proceeded towards the island, the calmer the sea became.

Within a quarter of an hour they made the leeward side of Cenotaph Island and dropped anchor. The ship still rocked a bit but the waves and wind were tolerable. Here she would spend the night.

The captain leaned back in his chair and lit his pipe. He didn't like being in Lituya Bay. While it provided good protection from the storm, it had an ominous reputation. He knew the stories; twice a tsunami had generated waves hundreds of feet high, once in 1854 and the most recent in 1899. Those that plied the waters of Alaska were well aware of the last incident. The wave was two-hundred feet high with the potential to destroy any ship in the bay. These incidents were rare, but the superstitious nature of most captains made them uneasy any time they were forced to take refuge here. In the end, the captain smiled to himself, happy to take the shelter and risk the improbable.

* * *

The passengers sensed something was happening when the ship turned hard to starboard. Their anxiety rose with the pounding of the engines. Those with a window or porthole peered out, straining to see where the ship was headed. With the wind and waves whipping up spray high in the air it was impossible to tell they were entering Lituya Bay. The surging and swinging of the bow further terrified the passengers, but they eventually realized the ship was not being buffeted nearly as much and the sea seemed a bit calmer. By the time they reached the island in the middle of the bay, the captain had sent stewards around to inform everyone they were safe and would be at anchor until the morning.

After an unsettling nights sleep, the morning broke fair and calm. The storm had blown itself out and the sea looked as flat as the proverbial mill pond. Most of the passengers were jolted awake by the *Northwestern* weighing anchor, the sound of the heavy chain grinding over the winch, sending vibrations throughout the ship.

Emily had recovered from her seasickness overnight and was feeling much better, especially given the change in the weather. They ate a light breakfast and watched as the ship headed back to the Gulf.

The captain timed their exit close to slack tide to avoid any further excitement for the passengers. With little to no current running, leaving Lituya Bay was uneventful. The ship turned to starboard and resumed its journey to Cordova. The waves were a bit higher once they left the protection of the bay, but the ship handled them with ease. The weather and sea conditions were a welcome relief to all on board.

The captain ordered full ahead and ship was making an easy eighteen knots through the relatively calm seas. At this rate, they would make Cordova in roughly seventeen hours, arriving late and in the middle of the night. *Oh well, it can't be helped,* the captain thought. His wasn't the first ship to be delayed by Alaska weather, and it wouldn't be the last.

Chapter 17

It took Thomas several hours to make his way back to town with his first moose. He took it slow, and several times had to dismount and lead the horse through some of the rougher terrain. Normally it would be no problem, but dragging a moose along behind them slowed their progress. He now understood why Wesley hunted with two horses.

As he approached the boarding house, he wondered how Stella would react. He'd been gone nearly two days. He could only imagine what she might be thinking, but he knew it wasn't good. It was nearly dark; he could see the lights burning in the kitchen.

He thought about going directly in, but decided to delay the inevitable by taking the horse around back. He led her to the small out building that was used to store various tools and also served as a place to hang meat to age. Seeing no sign of Stella, he proceeded to unlash the meat from the travois.

The building had ropes hanging from the beams, each with a metal hook on the end. Thomas took the first quarter into the building, hoisted it up, and hung it. He turned around to fetch the next one. Stella was standing in the doorway.

"You're back," she said in a strange tone of voice.

"I had some tr—"

"I was worried about you."

Before he could say anything, she stepped forward and grabbed him, hugging him like a mother bear. Then, letting go, she gently backhanded him across the shoulder.

"Don't do that to me again," she said, tears welling up in her eyes.

"I'm sorry, things just got out of hand and there was nothing I could do."

Thomas went on to explain to her everything that had happened, about wounding the moose, getting lost, the wolves, and finally making it back out. Stella listened intently while he finished hanging the moose and unpacked the wolf hides from the horse.

"Well, you've had quite an adventure," she said, sounding more like her old self. "But for me it brought back nothing but the worries of the past."

"I understand," he said. "I am truly sorry if I made you worry. I won't let it happen again."

"Good. Now finish up here and come in. I have some dinner waiting for you."

After a good nights sleep, Thomas spent the next day fleshing out the two wolf hides and salting them down to get them ready for the fur buyer. The moose was hanging, but it really was a little too warm to let it age for long. Thomas decided to deliver it and see about payment.

"Let's keep a bit of meat for us," said Stella as she entered the shed.

"Sure, what do you want?"

"The backstraps and tenderloins, of course," said Stella smiling.

Thomas obliged and removed the meat from the backbone along the rib cage.

"This will make for some good steaks," said Stella.

"I'll be ready when I get back from town," said Thomas, grinning widely as he loaded the moose meat and the hides into the wagon. With everything loaded up, he hitched up the horse and trotted off to the store.

* * *

"Well, I see you've done alright on your first hunt," said Noel Parker, looking over the moose in the wagon. "How was it?"

"I had a bit of trouble, but things worked out."

"Got a couple of wolves too I see. Those are mighty nice pelts. Sounds like you had quite a trip."

"I'll tell the story some time," said Thomas. "Can we settle up?"

Noel had Thomas take the wagon around back of the store where his small ice house was located. He sold ice in the summer and stocked it in the winter. The room was just cool enough to hang meat without spoilage until it could be processed or sold whole. Thomas helped Noel unload the wagon and hang the meat. As they brought each quarter in, Noel weighed it using the scale suspended from the ceiling. He recorded each weight on a scrap of paper he kept in his back pocket. When they were done, Noel tallied up the weights.

"Looks like you've got right around 450 pounds of moose there. Not a giant but certainly respectable," said Noel.

"What can you give me for it?"

"Well, we never talked price but I'll give you the going rate for moose on the hoof. Thirty cents a pound."

Noel scribbled on the pad of paper, working to figure out what he owed Thomas.

"That's 135 dollars," said Thomas.

Noel stopped scribbling and looked up. "Really?"

"I think so," said Thomas. "I was always pretty quick with figures."

Noel scribbled for a few more seconds and announced, "Uh... 135 dollars. By golly you're right! Let's go in and I'll get your money."

It seemed like a lot of money to Thomas, but he realized Noel planned to sell it for a lot more.

"We're expecting a shipment of beef soon," said Noel.

"Really?"

"Yeah, some of the companies put liquid ammonia refrigeration rooms in their steamships when they saw how much money could be had importing to the gold rush towns."

"I bet that's expensive," said Thomas.

"It is, but a lot of the miners prefer beef over wild game. On the other hand, I have a lot of customers that prefer fresh meat over beef that's been on a steamship for a week."

"That's good for me."

"Yeah, I never have trouble selling fresh game meat. Here you go," he said, handing Thomas a wad of cash. "What are you going to do with it?"

"Well, half of it goes to Stella. We're partners. Most of my share goes towards building up my grubstake so I can buy supplies and head to the Interior."

"Still have the gold mining dream do ya?"

"It's the reason I came up here and I plan to pursue it," said Thomas. "Right now I need a few things so I can do extended hunting trips."

"What do ya need?"

"Well, I have some cooking gear from Stella. What I really need is a small tent, a Mackinaw coat, and one of those heavy wool blankets," said Thomas, pointing at the shelf behind Noel.

"You're probably gonna want one of these oil blankets too. It'll help keep you dry at night."

"Throw one of those in too. Oh, and a gold pan. How much does that come to?" asked Thomas.

"Well, let's see here," Noel said as he worked at tallying up the items. "That's twenty-three dollars even. You want some mosquito netting too?"

"I guess I better have it as well," said Thomas. "How much do I owe you?"

"Mosquito netting is pretty cheap, let's just say twenty-four dollars and call it even. That work for you?"

"That's fine," said Thomas as he handed Noel forty dollars.

Noel took the money and set it on the counter while he ran back and forth collecting the items. He guessed at the size of coat and grabbed the tent last, plopping it down on the counter.

"Try the coat on to see if I guessed right."

Thomas slipped into the coat and it was a perfect fit. The heavy, water repellent material would keep him warm and dry. Noel flipped through the items on the counter to make sure he had everything. He picked up the two bills and paused.

"How about you give me those two wolf hides and we'll call it even?" he said, thrusting the money back at Thomas.

"Are you sure?"

"Yeah, it's a fair deal," said Noel with a wink.

Thomas thought for a moment. "Sure, you have a deal." He wasn't familiar with fur prices, but couldn't help wondering if there was a certain amount of charity involved in the transaction.

He gathered up his purchases and Noel followed him out the door to collect his pelts.

"Pleasure doing business with you," said Noel, straining under the weight of the wolf hides. "I'll have the moose sold out to the restaurants in no time so bring more anytime."

Thomas thanked him and climbed into the wagon. *One hundred and thirty-five dollars*, he marveled as he headed off to the boarding house.

* * *

Stella looked at the pile of cash Thomas dropped on the table and said, "Looks like Noel is paying more than when Wesley was hunting. How much is it?"

"A hundred and thirty-five dollars," said Thomas. "He's paying thirty cents a pound for moose."

"Well good for us. He'll sell it for a lot more so he's getting a good deal too," said Stella.

"I got the things I need for overnight trips too. I was all set to pay for them when Noel said he wanted my wolf pelts so I didn't have to lay out any cash."

"That worked out well. What do you say we keep the money all together and divide it when the time comes?"

He agreed that was acceptable. Stella took the money from the table and headed for the kitchen with Thomas in tow.

"What are you going to do with it?" he asked.

"I have a special place for things like this."

She opened a cupboard and took down an empty quart jar and lid. Taking the cash she rolled it up and put it in the jar and placed the lid on tightly.

"Move the wood box out from the wall for me."

Thomas looked at her for a moment to make sure he heard her right. She gave him the eye and he knew best to do as he was told. The box was heavy, being nearly full of wood for the cook stove. He tugged and pulled until it slid grudgingly from the wall, revealing what looked like a small hatch on the wall near the floor. Stella reached down and pried it open with her fingernail, exposing a small compartment and shelf. She placed the jar on the shelf and closed the hatch.

"You can slide the box back now."

Thomas slid the wood box back into place and waited for the story behind the hiding place.

"That's where Wes and I hid our valuables. You can never be too careful, especially with a lot of boarders coming and going. It's a safe place."

"You're right. I don't think many people would look there."

"Only two people know about it now," she said, smiling.

Content his fortune was safe, Thomas returned to the wagon and took care of Horse. He put the tent in the tool shed along with the blankets which he rolled tight and tied with some cord. He brought the coat and mosquito netting into the house, along with his pack—he had to get ready for his next trip and he wanted to leave soon.

* * *

Thomas was up before daylight, banging around in the tool shed trying to get all the camping gear assembled and ready to go. The cooking utensils were stored on the top shelf, in an ancient wooden box that once held something long forgotten. As he pulled the box from the shelf, he lost his grip. It went crashing to the floor, sending pots, pans, and silverware clattering all over the place.

Thomas swore under his breath. He had tried to keep quiet, knowing it was still early, even for Stella. Fortunately there were no neighbors nearby. He gathered up the mess and put everything back in the box. He would have to sort through it since there was much more than he intended to pack into the mountains.

Looking back at the house he could see the lamp was now burning in the kitchen. Sheepishly he returned to the house, box in hand and entered the back door.

"Good morning," said Stella. "I hear you've been busy this morning, what with all the racket you were making out back."

"Sorry," said Thomas. "I was trying to be quiet but I dropped this box full of kitchen things."

"You have plans for today?" she asked, knowing full well what was on his mind.

"I think I'm going to head back up and spend a night or two scouting about."

"I need to know how long you will be gone," she said. "So I know when to send out the search party."

She was trying to make light of it, but Thomas knew she was serious. It was a difficult situation. With so many things that could happen in the wilderness, sticking to firm timetables was near impossible.

"How about this; I plan to be gone two nights. Don't worry about me until after three."

"And you are going up Goat Creek?"

"Yes, but I want to keep my trail a secret. I'll tell you how to get there but let's not tell anyone unless absolutely necessary."

Thomas proceeded to explain to her how to get to the end of the established trail near the old cabin, then follow the river bed until the spruce wall.

"Once you get through the wall of spruce trees, the trail up the valley is easy to see," said Thomas.

Stella made note of the directions, hoping full well she wouldn't need them.

"I'm going up to my room to finish packing my gear."

"While you're doing that, I'll make you some coffee and breakfast. And you're going to need some food to take with you."

Thomas packed quickly. By the time he was done Stella had breakfast on. This morning's fare was fresh biscuits and gravy mixed with bear sausage. Thomas sat down and didn't even notice the fragrant smell drifting from his plate. He ate quickly while she stared at him, once again marveling at his lack of manners when he was on a mission.

"I have a couple of new boarders scheduled to arrive while you are gone," she said. "Miners headed the Fortymile I think. They'll only be here a couple of days."

"Good, glad to see you're getting some business" said Thomas. "Things have been kind of slow lately."

"Yes, most of them aren't even stopping here. Getting off the boat and making a run for it or camping out along the bay until they're ready to head for the hills."

Thomas briskly finished breakfast, grabbed his pack, and snatched up the food Stella had put together for his trip. He jaunted out the back door with Stella following behind. As he worked getting the horse packed and his gear stowed, Stella reminded him to be careful and made sure he understood she expected him back in two days. Of course he knew all this and couldn't help feeling like he was a young boy again with his mother instructing him before he went on his first hunting trip with his father.

"I've given you plenty of food so you shouldn't run out, as long as you're back on time," she said.

"Thanks. I will do everything in my power to be back on time," he said, grinning just a bit.

"You better take me seriously young man or you'll never get breakfast again."

"I will. Don't worry about me, I'll be fine," he said as he finished lashing down the gear and mounted up. "Just so you know, I plan to camp at the headwaters of the creek. I should be able to make it up there and still have time for some hunting today."

Satisfied her instructions had taken root, she said good-bye and Thomas rode off down the road towards the trail, just as the sun began to peek above the horizon.

Chapter 18

Most of the passengers were fast asleep when the *Northwestern* slipped quietly into its mooring in Cordova. The trip from Lituya Bay had been uneventful, with good weather all the way around. Time lost due to weather had put them almost a day behind; they should have been docking in Valdez by this morning. Now they would have to wait until daylight so the Cordova bound passengers could disembark and cargo could be unloaded. The captain expected to take on a few more passengers and some freight destined for Valdez, but now all that would have to wait until morning.

The captain figured they could make Valdez by late afternoon if they could get underway by mid-morning. It was a little less than ninety miles and with favorable weather it would take less than six hours. From Cordova the route would take them through Orca Bay into Prince William Sound and then on into Valdez Arm.

"Do you think we'll have any more trouble Captain?" asked the helmsman.

"If the weather holds we should be fine, the only thing to worry about is Bligh Reef. We need to be on watch, that reef has taken a lot of ships, going clear back to when the Russians were plying these waters," said the captain.

I hope the weather holds, thought the captain as he contemplated the route. At least the trip would be during daylight.

* * *

"I'm so excited I can't stand it!" said Emily, bursting into the cabin. "We're almost there!"

She had woken early to find they had made Cordova. In her excitement, she dressed quickly and went up on deck to survey the town, leaving her father still sound asleep. She breathed deeply, taking in the crisp morning air. Workers on the dock were just beginning to stir, slow to get started in the early morning light. She watched for a moment, but didn't stay long, rushing back to the cabin to share her excitement.

Her father sat straight up in bed, trying to get his bearings. "What—"

"We are in Cordova! I bet we will be leaving soon and then we will be there and I will see Thomas!"

This was the most emotion Emily had shown the whole trip. Any thought of sickness and shipwreck had evaporated. She was of a single mind now and her father knew it.

"Give me a minute so I can get dressed," he said.

Emily retreated, turning her back as John grabbed his clothes from the chair next to his bed. He dressed quickly and finished by smoothing his hair back with his hands.

"Well I'll be glad to get there and back on dry land," he said, as he stood up.

Emily turned. "Me too! Do you think it will take long to find him?"

"I don't know. It should be easy to find the boarding house, but we don't even know if he is still in Valdez."

This put an immediate damper on her enthusiasm. Her face drooped as the possibility of not finding Thomas sunk in, then quickly took on a scowl directed at her father.

"We really don't know if he has recovered or if he has moved on," said John. "I was hoping we would have received another letter or something before we left."

Emily slumped to her bed in a heap and began to cry. John sighed heavily, immediately realizing his mistake in being so brutal about the possibilities. Before they left Seattle he tried to lay out all the outcomes they might face. Now he realized her focus was so much on seeing Thomas she never even heard a word.

"Now, now," said John, attempting to repair the damage. "I'm sure we'll find him with no problem."

"But you said—"

"I know what I said, but I'm sure he is fine and I'll bet he is still in Valdez. A father knows these things," he said, smiling. He hoped she wouldn't detect the deception.

This seemed to calm Emily, but he wasn't sure. She dried her tears, wiping them unladylike with the back of her hand.

"Let's get something to eat and perhaps we can find out when we will be departing," said John.

Emily stood and straightened her dress, anxiety still painted on her face.

"Yes, Father. You must find out when we are leaving and how long it will take," she said coldly.

"I will," he said as he opened the cabin door and ushered her out. "Our breakfast awaits."

* * *

"Excuse me," said John, stopping the steward in the hallway just short of the stairs leading to the dining room.

"Yes sir?"

"Can you tell me when we will be departing for Valdez?"

"Sorry sir, I have no idea."

"Is there anyone who knows?"

"Just the captain, sir," said the steward as he slid past them in the narrow corridor and continued on his way.

He stopped two more stewards along the way, asking the same question. None of them knew anything.

John and Emily entered the dining room and found a table near a window. There were a few passengers sitting around, sipping coffee and talking about the events of the last two days.

"Coffee or tea for you?" asked the waiter as he placed the morning menu on their table.

"Coffee for me and tea for the young lady," said John. "And can you tell me when we will be leaving for Valdez?"

"No sir. But I will see if I can find out for you."

Finally someone that will at least try, he thought. John thanked him and he shuffled off, returning a minute later with coffee and tea.

"Are you ready to order?" he asked as he set their drinks on the table.

Emily hadn't looked at the menu. John decided to make the decision for her and ordered a simple breakfast of eggs and toast for them both.

"Thank you," said the waiter, retrieving the menus. "And I'm still trying to find out about our departure sir."

They sat there silently. Emily sipped her tea half-heartedly as she looked out the window. John was sorry he had been so blunt earlier.

"I wish mother were here," she said abruptly.

John didn't know what to make of that. Her mother was never in favor of this trip and had fought hard against it. John loved his wife, but having her on this trip would have frankly, made it unbearable. She would have complained about everything, from the quality of the food service to the weather. *God only knows how she would have reacted to being run aground.* John let Emily's statement pass.

The waiter returned with their food. "Here you are miss," he said as he sat her plate down. "And you sir."

"Thank you," said John. "Were you able to find out when we are leaving?"

"You are in luck sir. The captain happened to be in the galley with the first officer when I fetched your order. I overheard them saying we would be leaving by ten this morning."

"Did they say how long it would take?"

"No sir, but our run from Cordova to Valdez usually takes about six hours."

"Well that's good news," said John, thanking the waiter as he left.

They ate silently and awkwardly, Emily upset and John not knowing what to say.

Emily finally broke the silence. "How do we find the boarding house when we get there? What if we can't find it? And what if there is no place for us to stay? What will we do then?"

"Don't worry, I don't think we will have any trouble. It's a small town. We should be able to ask just about anyone for directions to the boarding house."

"And if there is no room for us where will we—"

"I'm sure there are a number of places to stay besides the boarding house. Don't worry, I'll take care of everything."

John noticed she hadn't mentioned finding Thomas since he had upset her. *Had she lowered her expectations?* He wished he had prepared her for the worst but he didn't know how to approach it. If Thomas hadn't recovered she would be devastated and there would be no consoling her. He wished he could find out beforehand and then break the news to her gently, but it was too late for that now.

* * *

The ship departed promptly at ten, steaming north before making the turn around Hawkins Island and heading across Orca Inlet. The captain had done his calculations and estimated they would be tied up at the dock in Valdez by three-thirty in the afternoon. Then it was unload passengers and cargo, take on more of the same, and depart for Seward—then turn around and do it all over again.

The weather was good and the majority of the passengers enjoyed the trip by going up on deck or sitting in the observation room. They were happy to be out of their cabins and out of the miserable seas that had plagued them in the Gulf.

Those disembarking at Valdez chatted happily at the prospect of completing their journey and being on solid ground again. Many were prospectors headed for the placer fields in the Interior. Others planned to prospect the sound for gold and copper. Those remaining on board were largely tourists who were now questioning their sanity and praying the rest of the trip would be less eventful.

Emily could hardly contain herself. Her mood had lightened as her thoughts turned to seeing Thomas. *I know he is alive and well*, she convinced herself, rehearsing the thought over and over in her mind. She had scurried up on deck and latched on to the rail, peering forward as if she could will the ship to go faster. The short trip to Valdez was taking an eternity, at least in her mind.

John on the other hand, sat back on a deck chair, smoking his pipe and watching Emily. He was at a loss for how to deal with what they might face in a few short hours. The letter said Thomas would recover. At least that's what the woman caring for him thought. John wondered, *Was she a doctor?*

"How much longer, Father?" Emily called from the railing without altering her gaze.

"Another two hours at least," John said, checking his pocket watch.

Emily turned from the rail and threw herself into the chair beside her father. "Oh! We'll never get there!" she said, pouting.

"Just like when you were a child at Christmas," said John, smiling. "You never had patience when you were excited."

"It's not funny," she said. "I'm excited and nervous at the same time."

"I suggest you relax. We'll be there soon enough and even then it is going to take some time to get off the ship and collect our belongings."

Emily reluctantly settled back in the chair, listening to the droning of the engines and the sound of the ship slipping through the gentle waves. As the sun warmed her face, she daydreamed of the reunion that had occupied her every waking moment.

Chapter 19

As he made his way to the spruce wall, Thomas thought about Stella, standing on the porch that morning, watching him as he rode out of sight. She had done so much for him, but at times he wanted to rebel at having another mother watching over him.

He dismissed the thought. Without her, who knows how things would have ended for him. The added burden of knowing her worries was something that nagged at him, but he resolved to do his best not to hurt her. After all, he cared for her.

When they reached the spruce wall, Thomas nudged the horse to the left so they would enter at a new spot. This, he hoped, would keep their trail from becoming worn and obvious to anyone passing by on the river bed. Once through, he let the horse pick its way up the trail while he scanned the valley for game.

He really didn't want to take anything yet, but rather wanted to complete his exploration of the head of the valley to see what might lie beyond. Still he thought it prudent to take note of where the moose were for future reference. As fate would have it, by the time they reached timberline he had seen nothing.

He stopped to water the horse by the creek as he scanned the valley walls. The sheep he had seen last time were nowhere to be found. *Perhaps they were on the back side of the mountain*, he thought.

As Thomas watched the horse drink, it occurred to him that he should try out his new gold pan. He fetched it and the short-handled shovel from the pack frame and stared at the creek, trying to decide where to dig. The horse paused her drinking and looked at him, water dripping from her chin, as if to question his actions.

Thomas thought back to the stories Haskell told about mining, remembering him mention that gold often accumulates on the downstream side of big boulders. Thomas found a good sized boulder next to the bank and decided to give it a try. He began digging, water swirling in the hole as he scooped out the first shovel full. He didn't know if he should pan it all or dig deeper. He decided deeper was better and threw the gravel on the bank, then proceeded to do the same several more times.

Satisfied he had got down to where the gold was---or might be, he loaded up his pan and stooped down next to the water.

Since he had never panned for gold, he tried to remember Haskell's description of the proper technique. He shook the pan back and forth to settle any gold to the bottom. Then, raking the bigger stones off the top, he proceeded to swirl the pan, working the top material off and adding water as needed.

Afraid of losing gold, Thomas worked very slowly. Twenty minutes later he was nearly to the bottom of his first pan. He swirled it slowly, tipping it up to reveal the nuggets he dreamed were there.

He was rewarded with no black sand, but several gold colored flakes, swirling in the pan. He jumped up and was about to let out a yell, when he noticed not only did the flakes swirl around in the water, several of them were floating on top. *I'm no mining engineer, but I'm pretty sure gold doesn't float.*

Thomas pulled out his knife and pressed the blade into one of the flakes. It split in two rather than flattening as gold would. Disgusted, he dumped the pan, realizing he had been tricked just as many before him. Gold colored mica wasn't going to make anybody rich. He shook the water off the gold pan and stowed it and the shovel back on the pack frame. *That was entertaining,* he thought. *Time to move on.*

Within minutes, they were approaching the head of Goat Creek. Thomas could see a low saddle, a pass that separated the drainage from whatever lie beyond the headwaters. If the descent into the valley below the pass was not too steep, it might open up into fertile hunting grounds.

The ascent to the saddle was rocky and a bit steep so Thomas chose to lead the horse to the top. There were trails worn into the talus slope that he assumed had been made by sheep. They did him little good however, as the trails traversed the saddle back and forth rather than providing a route up and over. The shale slipped beneath their feet, making the going slow and sometimes hazardous. Fortunately, the climb from the headwaters was only a couple hundred feet.

At the top, Thomas paused to catch his breath and survey the new valley before him. It opened up into a broad expanse, with several small lakes and what looked like good habitat for moose. The descent into the valley was gentle compared to the climb he had just made, making hunting it entirely possible.

Thomas smiled at his minor conquest. He wondered if anyone had been here before. The map Noel gave him didn't extend much beyond the mouth of Goat Creek. He had the feeling of a true pioneer, opening up a land of possibilities never seen before. Of course he had no way of knowing if anyone had been here—so far he had seen no evidence.

Thomas led the horse down into the new valley, picking his way among the large rocks that dotted the slope. There were no shale slides on this side, making the descent easy. Once in the valley, he decided to travel along the creek towards timberline. His goal was to find a campsite that afforded a good view of the entire valley. From there, he could glass the slopes and lakes to see if it was worth descending further to look for game.

Making his way down the valley was more difficult than it looked. From up top it looked all pleasant and green. Once in it, it was a maze of alder and willow which grew thick along the creek bottom. Walking down the narrow creek was an option, but the slippery boulders were just waiting to roll an ankle or send him face first into the water. Besides, the water was incredibly cold.

Thomas decided to cross the creek to see if it was easier going. At first it looked no better. He moved further away from the creek to see if the scrub willow would thin out. About twenty-five yards in, he picked up a game trail. It was worn deep into the ground, nearly a foot or so. The brush was not as thick as along the creek, making it easier to dodge the alder and willow that overhung the trail. Being in the thick brush made him uneasy. He pulled the .45-70 from its scabbard and carried it in one hand, leading Horse with the other.

An hour later he had made his way to a large, barren knoll above the creek. He was happy to be out of the brushy creek bottom and back where he could see down the valley. This would be a good spot to camp. He moved away from the creek, along the edge of the knoll, looking for an ideal spot to pitch his tent.

He topped a small rise on the knoll, just a few feet higher than the rest and saw a flat spot ahead. It looked like a promising camp site, but was a bit rocky. As he approached, Thomas saw the rocks were arranged in a circle. It was a fire ring.

* * *

Thomas stared at the circle and sighed, his illusion of being a pioneer shattered. Someone had used this valley before. The fire ring held only ashes and hadn't been used in a long time. Still his feeling of being a great explorer had vanished.

He set about unpacking the gear from the horse and setting up the tent. He removed the saddle and pack frame from the horse and tied her up to the long metal stake he was able to drive into the rocky ground. With the axe in hand, he walked a short distance to a small stand of spruce, the only real trees on the entire knoll. He gathered an armful of dry wood for a small fire, enough to cook some dinner and give a little warmth.

As he built the fire, he wondered who had been here in the past. There were no clues to be found in the fire pit or around the campsite. *Was it a traveler that stopped for a single night?*

It seemed like a lot of work to root these rocks out of the ground or carry them all the way from the creek bottom to make a fire ring for one night. No, this must have been a campsite used more than once. *But for what purpose,* he wondered.

Once the fire was going strong, Thomas made some coffee. Coffee never kept him from sleep, besides, he was tired and didn't feel like cooking anything. Instead he ate jerky and some of the bread Stella had packed for him. He stared out across the valley as the sun set slowly behind the mountains. The fire faded as Thomas retreated into the tent and crawled under the wool blanket. Before darkness enveloped the valley, he was asleep.

Chapter 20

As soon as the town of Valdez came into sight, Emily was back at the rail, peering forward one minute and chattering excitedly to her father the next. They were close now, steaming east through Port Valdez. Though still over five miles away, the town was clearly visible in the distance. With each minute Emily grew more animated. John, on the other hand, found himself pacing the deck, his anxiety increasing at the thought of what they might learn once there.

Their bags were already packed; Emily had insisted on packing right after breakfast to make sure there was no delay in disembarking the ship. She was adamant they find Thomas today. John tried to explain that by the time they made it off the ship and collected their belongings it may be too late too look for him. After all, they had to find a place to stay as soon as possible. Emily was not the camping type and of course they had made no preparations in that regard anyway. Emily largely ignored him and was still intent on finding Thomas.

The sun had already dipped behind the mountains as the *Northwestern* eased into the dock at Valdez. Immediately, even before she was tied up, the passengers began crowding towards the gang planks to exit the ship. Emily had her bag over her shoulder and was pushing her way through the crowd in a most uncharacteristic way. John was behind her, apologizing for his daughter and trying to get her to refrain from being rude.

"We need to get off the ship and get going!" she half-shouted to her father as he struggled to keep up with her.

"Calm down," said John, firmly putting his hand on her shoulder. "You are acting like a spoiled child."

Embarrassed, Emily stopped and turned to her father,

trying to hide from the eyes of the other passengers.

"I'm sorry," she said, her head down, looking at the deck. "It's just I am so anxious I'm beside myself."

"I know. But we have to do things in a proper manner. Once we get off the ship we'll collect our luggage and find a place to stay."

"Can we find Thomas today?"

"If we have time. But I'm not about to go roaming around a strange town in the dark, especially with you along."

Emily didn't like what she heard, but she accepted her father's decision. *After all, it doesn't make sense to go wandering around at night.* She resigned herself to take things as they came; still, she would try and wrap her father around her little finger when the time came.

"Come, the line is moving now," said John.

* * *

It took longer to disembark than expected. Even after they were off the ship, there was a delay in offloading luggage. Emily paced back and forth on the dock while they waited. John stood by, trying to get a glimpse of each bag as it was carried ashore. All the passengers were standing around, waiting for unloading of the bags to be complete; only then would they be able to claim them. The bags were placed in a holding area and there were a couple of rather large agents standing nearby.

John regarded the process as somewhat odd, but also realized there may be a substantial criminal element operating in this frontier town. He checked his inside vest pocket to make sure his wallet was secure.

Finally, passengers were allowed to begin claiming their luggage, presenting their ticket stubs as confirmation. The two large men checked to ensure all bags were properly claimed. John located their luggage, a large steamer trunk and two smaller bags. It was more than he could carry at one time. He drug the trunk over near one of the agents and motioned for Emily to come and wait with it. Then he retrieved the other bags and presented their tickets to the agent. He checked the bags without saying anything, grunted his approval, and motioned for them to move along. John handed Emily the smaller bag and he managed to wrestle the trunk and the other bag away from the dock and towards the street. They needed transportation.

On the street there were a few small wagons and drivers lined up, waiting for a fare. To John, they looked a little shady, but he had little choice. Before he and Emily reached the street, each began yelling to them, trying to win their business. That quickly deteriorated into yelling and cursing at each other, arguing about who saw them first. Fortunately, other passengers from the ship reached the street and the competition ended. John hailed the wagon at the head of the line and lugged the trunk towards it, Emily following close behind. The driver jumped down and ran towards them.

"Let me help you with that, sir," said the driver. "Name's Billy, what's yours?"

John took stock of the man before him. Billy looked to be in his mid-twenties. His long hair was protruding from under his wrinkled hat and he looked and smelled like he could use a long bath. With lye soap.

"I'm John and this is my daughter Emily," he said extending his hand.

Billy shook his hand and looked past him, staring at Emily longer than a father should allow. Embarrassed and a bit frightened, she looked down, breaking the spell.

"Here, let's get that trunk in my wagon. And give me

your bag Emily," said Billy.

He helped John carry the trunk to the wagon and tossed the bag in after it.

"Let me help you up miss," Billy said, reaching for her arm.

"That's fine," said John. "I'll help her."

John was not a suspicious person by nature, but already he was on guard. He helped Emily up into the seat and then climbed up next to her.

"Where to?" said Billy.

"We're here to find my fianc—"

"Do you know where Stella Baird lives?" asked John, interrupting Emily before she shared too much information.

"Stella? Yeah, she has a place a ways out of town. Got a plot of land there up towards the canyon and a boarding house. That where you're going?"

"How far is it?" asked John.

"Oh, about five or six miles."

"Why does she have a boarding house that far out of town?" asked John.

"Well, it's kind of a good place to stay for people moving farther north. Kinda get a head start on the competition if you know what I mean," said Billy.

Emily was on the edge of her seat. Watching and listening intently to see what her father had planned.

"Do you think she would be able to put us up for the night?" asked John.

"No way of telling."

"How long would it take to get to her place?"

"Oh, probably a little over an hour. The trail's still in rough shape from breakup so it's slow going in a lot of places," said Billy.

"What's breakup?" asked Emily.

"You know, the snow melts, frost goes out, and everything turns to mud and ruts."

"Is there a hotel in town?" asked John.

"Yeah, we got a couple."

John looked at his watch. If they went out to the boarding house and there wasn't room, they would have a long ride back in the dark. Then they risked not getting a room in town as things filled up for the night. He knew Emily wasn't going to be happy, but it was the wise thing to do.

"Take us to the nicest hotel in town," said John, watching the expression on Emily's face turn from hope to resignation.

"You bet," said Billy. "I'll have you there in no time."

* * *

The best hotel in Valdez was not at all what Emily expected. It was plain, a two-story building covered with rough hewn siding. *At least it wasn't a log cabin*, she thought. Billy did as little as possible to earn his fare. He watched as John dragged the trunk to the door of the hotel, then stuck out his hand waiting to be paid. John paid him, but gave him nothing extra. He didn't particularly like the man and his repeated stares at Emily.

The hotel lobby was plain and furnished sparsely. There were few decorations about, apart from a framed photograph of miners standing next to a sluice box and a large set of moose antlers over the fireplace. *Not up to par with Seattle, but it will do*, thought John.

After sharing a cabin on the ship the entire way, John decided to let his daughter have some privacy for a change and rent two rooms. He hoped he could get rooms on the first floor to avoid dragging the trunk up a set of stairs. The clerk looked up from the counter as they entered.

"Need a room?" asked the clerk.

No, I just like dragging this trunk from place to place, thought John. He nearly voiced it, but decided against it. It had been a long day and to his surprise, he was becoming a bit grumpy.

"I would like two rooms please."

"You're in luck," said the clerk. "I have two left, one downstairs and one up. Big bed in each."

"Nothing on the same floor?" asked John.

"Nope, sorry. Place fills up fast when a boat comes in."

He didn't like being separated from his daughter, but John had little choice, especially since the rooms had only a single bed.

"Alright, I'll take them both," he said.

"Sign in then," said the clerk turning the registry around. "Just sign once and I'll put the room numbers next to your name."

John wrote their names in the registry. The clerk spun the book back around and wrote room numbers next to each.

"I put the young lady in room twenty upstairs and you in room seven sir. That work for you?"

John thought for a second and decided Emily would be safer upstairs than down. "Yes, that's fine," he said.

The clerk handed them the keys. "Have a good night folks."

John dragged the trunk to his room, unlocked the door and shoved it and his bag inside. Locking the door, he took the remaining bag from Emily.

"Let's take this to your room Emily," he said as he headed up the stairs.

Emily followed, being careful not to snag her dress on the rough lumber of the stairway. *Mother would call this hotel rustic,* she thought to herself.

They made it to the top of the stairs and followed the long narrow hallway until they found her room. John unlocked the door and let her in. He followed and sat the bag down next to the bed. The room was small and had a single window facing the street. Emily surveyed the room and then looked at her father.

"This is worse than what we had on the ship," she said. "I don't want to stay here."

"It's just for one night I hope," said John. "Tomorrow we will go out to the boarding house and see if we can find Thomas. If we're lucky, Mrs. Baird will have room for us and things will hopefully be more comfortable."

"Oh, that would be wonderful!" said Emily. The thought of seeing Thomas tomorrow made the drab room seem not so bad. "I hope we can stay there."

"I know it will be difficult, but I want you to get plenty of rest tonight. Lock your door after I leave and don't open it for anyone but me."

Emily looked worried. "Are you trying to scare me Father? Because it's working."

"I'm sorry. It's just that we are in a strange town and don't know our way around. I just want you to be safe. You'll be fine," he said as he turned to leave. He stopped, returned and gave her a kiss on the cheek.

"Now lock the door and get some rest. I'll come up and get you in the morning."

"Goodnight, Father," said Emily as he shut the door behind him. Emily locked the door and sat down on the bed. Tomorrow she would see Thomas. She wondered if he was well, and smiled as she thought about how surprised he was going to be when he saw her.

She readied herself for bed, folding her clothes neatly and laying them across the chair next to the bed. She pulled a dress for her reunion from the bag and tried to press the wrinkles out. What she really needed was an iron, but that was not to be. She straightened the dress and hung it up, hoping most of the wrinkles would be gone by morning.

The bed wasn't very comfortable, but she pulled the wool blanket up to her neck and closed her eyes. Sleep didn't want to come; she was too anxious about tomorrow. Starting from the beginning, she recounted how they met, how infatuated she was with him from the beginning, and the way in which she had fallen in love.

As the thoughts floated gently through her mind, she fell asleep.

* * *

John awoke at six o'clock. He was hungry, especially since they hadn't eaten since leaving the ship. In his haste to find accommodations the night before, dinner had been sacrificed. John went to the front desk and found it empty. There was no bell to ring. He looked through the doorway behind the counter to see the clerk slumped in a chair, snoring loudly. He hesitated for a moment, then decided to wake him, knocking on the counter top as hard as he could.

The clerk jerked awake, almost tipping the chair over backwards. Mumbling under his breath, he stumbled from the back room and made it to the counter.

"Yeah?" he said with his eyes barely open.

"Good morning," said John, smiling widely. "Where can we get something to eat? Is anything open this early?"

"Well, there is the bar down the street, but they don't open till later. Then there is Millie's place. I think they should be open by seven. What time is it anyway?"

"A little after six," said John.

"You're an early riser. You checking out this morning?"

"Yes, I believe we will, but after breakfast."

"Okay, I'll be here," said the clerk as he returned to the back room and slid into the chair.

John admired the clerk's ability to fall asleep so easily. Returning to his room, he pulled out his pocket watch. *Another forty-five minutes till Millie's opens.* He decided to let Emily sleep for another half hour or so, then wake her to get ready for breakfast. He packed the few things he had removed from the small bag and tossed it on top the trunk. Pulling up the nearby chair, he put his feet up on the bed and lit his pipe. *Just enough time for a smoke before breakfast*, he thought.

Just before seven, John climbed the stairs and walked the hall to Emily's room. He knocked quietly on the door. No answer. He knocked louder and called her name. Still no answer. He grabbed the knob and turned. To his surprise, the door was unlocked. He couldn't believe it. *After my lecture last night she left the door unlocked?* He opened the door and entered, calling her name.

His eyes shot to the bed. It was made and her bag was on the floor nearby. Emily however, was gone.

Chapter 21

Thomas awoke as the first rays of light began to streak across the sky. He thought about laying there a while, tucked under the warm wool blanket rather than crawling out into the cold morning air. After a few moments, he decided coffee sounded better than the hard ground pressing into his back. He threw the wool blanket aside, donned his coat, and exited the tent.

Overnight the fire died. Thomas scraped through the coals with a stick to see if there was any heat left, but found it stone cold. He took what was left of the wood, split it, and built a little pyramid in the fire pit. The dead branches from a nearby spruce provided the needed kindling. In short order he had a small fire going and coffee brewing. He thought about cooking something for breakfast, but decided against it. He was on a tight schedule and taking time to cook didn't appeal to him—at least not his first morning out. Bread and jerky would do for breakfast.

As he sat on the hillside looking out across the valley he cradled the steaming cup of coffee in his hands. The warmth felt good in the cool morning air. He surveyed the terrain below him, working out his plan for the day. Since he promised Stella to return tomorrow, he didn't dare venture too far down the valley. He decided to leave the camp up and use it for another night. From here, he could easily make it back by dark tomorrow. With that bit of logistics settled in his mind, he set about devising a route for exploring the valley.

Following the creek seemed to be the best choice, even though it would mean skirting patches of alder now and then. He hoped to pick up another game trail that would make travel easier. There was time to take a moose if he could do it early in the day. He thought about leaving the horse behind, but that would complicate things if he was successful on the hunt.

Downing the last of the coffee, Thomas packed up the things needed for the day. The horse seemed ready to move on, more likely anxious to get to the creek for a drink. He took a good look around at the landmarks. The last thing he wanted to do was lose the camp and spend the night sleeping on the ground again. Satisfied he had his bearings, Thomas took off down the knoll, headed for the creek with Horse in tow.

* * *

It was slow going at first. Thomas marveled at how the alders could grow in a tangle instead of up and down like normal trees. After watering Horse downstream from the camp, they moved away from the creek looking for the game trail from the night before. After stumbling through Devil's Club and alder for a hundred yards or so, the trail appeared. Though it made walking easier, the overhanging trees meant Thomas had to walk rather than ride. Even so, he made good progress and in an hour the trail had taken them to a spot where the creek widened and the trees gave way to a large open area.

The sun cleared the east side of the valley and Thomas felt the warmth growing as he walked along the creek. He decided to explore downstream a bit on his own.

"You stay here old gal," he said as he tied Horse off to a fallen tree near the creek. She could graze in the grass of the meadow and have access to water while he was gone.

Thomas took the .45-70 and his pack and headed downstream along the creek. The walking was easy here. The noise of the creek was just loud enough to drown out the sounds of the forest. He walked slowly, looking for sign and taking in the solitude of the valley. As he rounded a bend in the creek he could see the sandbar had been disturbed. Drawing closer it became clear; they were tracks—big bear tracks, and they were fresh. Thomas put his foot next to the hind track. It was longer than his boot. A chill ran up his spine. *This is no black bear.*

From the tracks, Thomas could tell the bear crossed the creek and was headed in the same direction he was going. He racked a round into the chamber of the .45-70 and continued down the creek. Shooting a big grizzly wasn't really in his plans. He doubted he could sell the meat and it seemed more trouble than it was worth to come back with just a hide—plus he didn't relish the idea of a run-in with the huge beast.

You leave me alone and I'll leave you alone bear, thought Thomas as he pushed forward down the creek. There were only a few hours remaining before he had to head back to camp. Picking his way along the creek, he looked for moose sign while keeping an eye out for bears. He wanted to cover as much ground as possible and quickened his pace.

The meadow gave way to a long stretch of thick alder and willow. Thomas found himself searching for a way through the tangle without wading the creek. Getting wet didn't sound appealing. He fought his way through the brush and away from the creek. The game trail he followed earlier was nowhere to be found. Through the brush he could see an opening ahead. Crawling his way through the maze, he broke out into the clear.

Sweat trickled down his forehead as he stopped at the edge of the clearing to catch his breath. He wiped his face with his handkerchief and pulled the canteen from his pack. As he tipped it back to take a drink, something in the middle of the clearing caught his eye. The sun was glinting off a single bright object barely visible in the grass. Thomas closed the canteen, sat the pack down, and headed into the clearing. At ten feet it became clear what he was seeing. It was a skull.

* * *

Thomas stopped and took a deep breath. With the grizzly prowling the valley he was already a little tense. He wondered if this was a bear kill but then quickly realized he was being silly. It obviously wasn't recent. It takes a while for bones to become bleached. From where he was standing he couldn't tell what sort of animal it was. *Must be a moose,* he thought. He moved forward to investigate.

The grass was tangled and woven, the spring growth mixed with the old and dry. Even so, the skull was clearly visible. Thomas approached and saw it was upside down with the lower jaw gone. It had been there long enough to settle into the ground an inch or two. Thomas kicked at it and flipped it over. Slowly he realized what it was—a bear skull. He had never seen a grizzly skull and this was huge. It obviously belonged to a very large bear. Setting the .45-70 gently in the grass, he picked it up for a closer look. The teeth were impressive; long curved and still very sharp. This didn't help calm his nerves any.

Thomas heard a noise directly behind him. He dropped the skull and spun around to see a raven fluttering to a landing in the tall spruce several yards behind him. The raven gave him a sideways look, decided there was nothing to be scavenged, and flew off. Thomas picked up the rifle and decided to keep it in hand. He was glad no one was around to see how jumpy he was.

Turning back towards the skull, he surveyed the scene. No other bones were visible. *Must have been dragged off by scavengers*, he thought. He moved forward slowly, sweeping his foot back and forth to clear the grass. He was only about five feet from where the skull was laying when his foot struck something deep in the grass. Kneeling down he tore through the mat and saw decaying wood and then metal. He grabbed the metal and pulled it free from the tangle. It was a rifle. As it came free it revealed something else; another skull. A human skull.

Chapter 22

John stood looking at the empty room, panic welling up inside him. He tried to suppress all the thoughts flooding his mind. *Where was she? Had someone taken her?* He could see Lydia collapsing in shock as he told her their daughter was lost in Alaska, never to be found again. Then would come the blame, the "I told you so," and the guilt. He snapped back to the present. He had to find her now.

He raced down the stairs to the front desk. The clerk was still asleep. John pounded on the counter, "Wake up!"

The clerk nearly fell over backwards in his chair as he was jolted awake.

"Wha—"

"Have you seen my daughter?" John asked, leaning over the counter, fists clenched.

"I ain't seen nobody," said the clerk. "You're the only one who keeps waking me up."

"My daughter is not in her room and the door was unlocked. Did you see anybody go upstairs last night after we arrived?"

"Nope. You was the last ones to get here last night."

"And no one has checked out this morning?"

"Not that I seen."

"Well keep an eye out for her and if she comes back tell I said to wait in her room."

"I'll try," said the clerk. "If I'm awake when she comes in."

John turned from the counter in disgust and stepped out onto the porch of the hotel. Even though it was early, there were a few people on the street. The sun was already above the horizon and the fog that had rolled in overnight was rapidly burning off. John wasn't sure what to do. Emily had always been a bit impetuous, but rarely did anything to cause him and Lydia concern. That's what troubled him so much about her disappearance.

As he started up the street, a horse and wagon approached. John hailed the driver.

"Have you seen a young girl on the street this morning?"

"What kind of girl you looking for mister," said the seedy looking driver, winking with a twisted grin.

John sneered at the man and swore. "She's my daughter and she's missing."

"Ain't seen nothing," said the driver as he slapped the reins and rolled away.

Frustrated, John continued briskly toward the restaurant, stopping everyone he could, asking if they had seen Emily.

By the time he reached Millie's, the open sign was hanging in the window. He quickly poked his head inside to see if perhaps Emily was there. The place had a few rough looking characters sitting around hunched over coffee. John motioned for the waitress to come over.

"What can I help you with hon?" she said.

"My daughter is missing from our hotel room. She is nineteen years old. Has she been in here this morning?"

"Sorry, I haven't seen anybody in here this morning except these greenhorn miners," she said, motioning towards the nearest table. "Maybe she went for a walk. It's a nice morning."

"Maybe," said John. "Thank you," he said as he left Millie's and headed up the street.

It started deep in his stomach, and welled up into his

throat. That feeling of panic and helplessness, trying to overcome him. He pushed it aside and walked quickly up the street, looking back and forth as he passed each building, searching for Emily. If he didn't find her soon he was going to have to find help.

Halfway up the street he noticed the building on his left had the door propped open. It was the local general store. Reaching the door, he saw Emily, facing away from him and talking excitedly with her hands to a man behind the counter.

"Emily," he shouted, his voice stern as he entered the store.

"Oh, Father," she said, spinning around. "This man knows Thomas and saw him just the other day," she said excitedly.

"Where have you been? I have been looking all over for you. You had me scared to death."

"I couldn't sleep so I got up early and took a walk. Then I got to thinking maybe Thomas would come to town so I started looking for him."

"You shouldn't have left the hotel. This town isn't at all like our neighborhood in Seattle."

"I'm fine. Mr. Parker was telling me about Thomas and where he is staying," she said, barely able to contain her excitement.

"That's nice. But don't you ever do that again. On this trip you will stay with me and I will know where you are at all times. Do you understand?"

"Yes, Father. I'm sorry, but I just am so excited to finally see Thomas."

No matter how frustrated he was with her imprudent behavior, John just couldn't stay mad at her—for long. He stepped past Emily and thrust out his hand to the man across the store counter. "

Name is John, John Palmer," he said, shaking the man's hand.

"I'm Noel. Welcome to my establishment," he said, returning the gesture.

"So you know Thomas? Is he well?"

"He is doing fine. Miss Stella got him back on his feet and they started a business venture together."

"Oh, they are mining together?"

"No, Father, he is hunting and selling the wild game to Mr. Parker," said Emily.

"That's right. He's just getting started. Brought me in a moose a few days ago."

John was relieved Thomas was alive and apparently doing well. "Is he in town?"

Noel thought for a moment. "I can't say for sure. I think he was bound and determined to head back up to his new hunting spot and do some more scouting around. Stella will know what he's up to. She keeps a close watch on him. Kinda like the son she never had," said Noel, smiling slightly.

"We plan to head out to her place after breakfast. Do you think she will have room to put us up?"

"Well, from what I hear, things have been a bit slow at the boarding house lately so I'll bet she has some room."

"What's the best way to get out to her place?" asked John as Emily fidgeted next to him.

"You can get one of the guys with a wagon to take you out there," said Noel.

"We got a ride from the dock to the hotel with a fellow named Billy," John said. "I guess we could see if he could take us out there."

"I hate to speak ill of folks, but I'd stay away from

him if I were you."

"Really? I know I didn't care much for the way he was eyeing my daughter," said John as he glanced at Emily. She was blushing.

"Yeah, he's known for being trouble. I suspect he's been involved in a lot more than we know, but I couldn't prove it," said Noel.

"We'll steer clear of him," said John.

"Just get Nate down at the hotel to get someone to take you out to Stella's," said Noel.

"Is he the sleepy little man behind the counter?"

Noel laughed. "Yeah, that's him. He's an okay guy, just a bit lazy now and then," he said, chuckling.

"Emily, let's go get some breakfast, then we'll check out of the hotel and see if we can find Thomas."

Emily nearly jumped up and down at her father's words and burst out the door.

"I better catch up," said John, smiling. "Thanks for your help Mr. Parker."

"Call me Noel," he said as John headed out the door to catch up with his daughter.

* * *

"Found her, eh?" said the waitress at Millie's.

"Yes, you were right. She took an early morning walk," said John as she seated them at a corner table.

The place was filling up as transients and town's folk ambled in for breakfast. John had to nearly twist Emily's arm to get her to even consider eating something. He loved her but she was nearly unbearable in her obsession to find Thomas. He remembered something of that type of passion from years ago. It saddened him a bit to realize it had long faded from his own marriage.

"I'm Sarah," said the waitress. "What brings you two to our little slice of heaven on earth?" she said, rolling her eyes and smiling.

John introduced himself and Emily, but before he could politely answer her question, Emily began to tell her life story, at least the part involving her and Thomas.

"Oh, you're looking for that fella that was shot a while back. Fine looking man. If I was just a few years younger..."

Emily frowned and John nearly laughed out loud.

"You know him?" said Emily sternly.

"Not really. He doesn't spend much time in town. I've seen him about and of course most people in town know who he is, just because of what happened."

"What did happen?" asked John.

"All I know is he got off the boat and within no time someone had put a bullet in him and robbed him. I think he nearly died but a couple of the boys gathered him up and took him out to Stella Baird's place so she could patch him up."

"But he is okay?" asked Emily.

"Looks fine to me," said Sarah, winking at John.

"Hey! Can ya quit your yacking and get us some coffee over here?" yelled one of the locals two tables over.

"Yeah, yeah, I'm coming," said Sarah. "I'll be back to get your order in a minute," she said as she sauntered off to fetch some coffee.

"I don't like her," said Emily flatly.

"Why not?" asked John, playing along.

"I don't like the way she talks about Thomas. I think she's forward."

"Oh, I don't know. Thomas could do worse."

"Father! How could you say something like that?"

"I'm just teasing you Emily. And so was the waitress. Don't take things so seriously."

"Well, I don't think it's funny."

Sarah returned to take their order. Emily fixed her gaze on the table and didn't look up or speak.

"What can I get you?"

"Just give us toast and eggs over easy. Coffee for me and some tea for my daughter if you have it."

"No problem, John," said Sarah smiling as she sashayed off.

"I told you she was forward," said Emily. "And she's old."

John thought it funny how at nineteen, anyone over thirty was old. Sarah brought their food and plopped it quickly on the table. Things were getting busy and she had no time left for casual conversation.

John finished a bite and placed his fork on the plate. "Emily, I'm still quite upset with your behavior this morning."

Emily looked up, eyes wide and mouth half open.

"You ignored my warning to stay in your room. How do you think I felt when I opened the door and found you gone?"

"I'm sorry, but—"

"It's not acceptable. I know you are an adult, but you will listen to me from now on."

"Are you mad at me, Father?" she said, her eyes reddening.

"No Emily. The lecture is over, now let's forget it and move on. We have a young man to find today."

Emily smiled. "Thank you Father."

"Anything else?" asked Sarah as she paused at their table.

"No, thank you," said John. "Just the check."

"Here ya go," she said as she slapped it down. "You can pay me when you're ready."

John already had his wallet out. He looked at the check and marveled at how high the prices were here. He hoped he had brought enough money to sustain them.

"Here you are," he said handing her enough to cover the meal and a bit more for a tip.

"Well, thank you sir," she said, bowing slightly. "You can come back and see me anytime, John," she said in a sing-song voice, winking at him and smiling as she walked away.

Emily just shook her head. "Let's go, Father. I've had enough of this place for today."

"Right," said John, smiling. "Let's head back to the hotel, check out, and see if we can't arrange some transportation out to Stella's."

"Now we're getting somewhere," said Emily, clapping her hands together silently. "Let's go."

Chapter 23

The hollow eyes of the skull stared back at Thomas, the dark remnant of a life once lived. Thomas had never seen human remains before. This find, in the middle of a wilderness, was the most unnerving thing he had ever experienced.

Suddenly the place transformed from meadow to memorial. Thomas knelt on one knee and tried to grasp the struggle of life and death that had taken place so far from civilization. It was primal. It was the most elemental of things one can experience. Man alone against nature and yet here, both had lost. If anyone had been with him, Thomas would have found himself speechless.

Thomas tried to stitch together what had happened. It seemed fairly obvious the man had shot the bear and the bear had attacked. What wasn't clear was which came first. Was the bear shot intentionally and then it charged? Or had the bear charged and the hunter shot in defense. It really didn't matter; the outcome was the same. Both had died in this remote place. Thomas wondered how he would react when put to the same test. He didn't want to find out.

He looked at the rifle. The barrel was rusted badly and the stock had begun to break down from exposure to the elements. He rubbed some of the rust off the barrel, trying to determine what kind of rifle it was. Near the breech he found what he was looking for, stamped into the metal. It was a Winchester Model 1876.

The hair on the back of his neck stood up and his pulse quickened. With his heart pounding Thomas searched for anything that might have belonged to the person that was now just a skull. There, not far from the remains, he found a pocket watch deep in the grass. It had stopped long ago. Turning it over he found a simple inscription: *W.B.*

His fears were confirmed. He had found Wesley.

* * *

Thomas sat there for a long time, staring. *I should say some words*, he thought, but didn't really know what to say. He believed in God, but rarely relied on his faith. Now he wished he could say something meaningful, even if only for his own comfort.

His thoughts turned to Stella. *How can I possibly tell her?* Furthermore, he didn't know what to do with the remains. Should he bury them here where Stella would never visit, or return them to her for a proper burial? He thought about burying Wesley and returning the rifle and watch to her. It was a problem he wished he didn't have to solve. Either way he had to deal with the remains.

He began to search, sweeping the grass away and looking for anything else belonging to Wesley. He found shreds of clothing, but nothing intact. He began walking a circular pattern, extending further from the kill site with each pass.

It was remarkable how so little could be left. But after all, it had been five years since Wesley disappeared. He found the sole of a boot about fifteen feet from where he found the rifle. Nearby he found a single bear claw in a small open patch of ground. After an hour he had searched the entire meadow with no success. He found no other bones; the predators had seen to that.

Thomas thought long and hard about his options. Whatever he did would be carefully thought out to make it as easy as possible on Stella. *Easy on Stella,* he thought. No matter what he did it wasn't going to be easy for her.

I must take everything back.

From his pack, Thomas removed a bandana. He carefully placed it over what remained of Wesley and wrapped it gently. He placed the remains in the pack along with the pocket watch. There was room in the pack for the bear skull but somehow it didn't seem right. He lashed it and the Winchester to the outside of the pack with a length of small cord. Next he set about marking the place.

Thomas had left the axe at the camp. All he had with him to make a marker was a hunting knife. At the edge of the clearing he searched for alder branches that were straight. He found a suitable tree and carved his way through the two inch branch, cutting a length about five feet long. Using the knife Stella had given him, a knife once belonging to Wesley, he cut a section from the branch from which to fashion a cross. He notched both pieces and bound them together with some of the cord. Taking the knife, he sharpened the end of the cross and then pushed it into the soft ground of the meadow, at the very spot where he had found Wesley.

Standing there in the silence of the moment, he felt great sadness. He did not know this man, but he knew the woman that loved him. It was a feeling of loss that surprised him, but yet he felt deeply. "I will never forget this place," he said as he turned from the cross and headed back through the alder maze.

Chapter 24

John had to practically run to keep up with his daughter after leaving Millie's for the hotel. He understood her excitement. It had been a trying journey for her and she could see the end in sight. They now knew Thomas was alive and doing well. John assumed all that remained in Emily's mind was to find him and head back to Seattle. *I'm not so sure it will be that easy*, thought John as they entered the hotel.

Nate was now fully awake, having had to deal with customers checking out. John nodded at him as he approached the desk. Nate half-smiled, or was it a frown? John wasn't sure. *He is an odd one*, thought John. *Seemed to be a lot of that in this town.*

"Can you arrange for a wagon to take us and our things out to Stella's boarding house as soon as possible?"

"Sure. I'll keep an eye out for the next fella to go by and flag him down. Some of the guys should be heading for the dock soon."

"That's fine, but I don't want Billy," said John.

"Oh? You don't like him?"

"Let's just say I would rather give my money to someone else."

"Okay, okay. I'll get one of the other fellas for you. How soon will you be ready to leave?"

"As soon as we get our things from the room and check out."

"I'll see what I can do," said Nate.

John escorted Emily to her room to fetch her things. She had already packed before going on her morning adventure, but now she was wondering if she should change before she saw Thomas.

"Do you think this dress looks nice enough?"

"Yes, I think it looks fine."

"But I want to look special when I see Thomas. I need the blue dress from the trunk."

"Fine," said John. "Let's take your bag downstairs and I'll wait by the front desk while you change in my room."

"Oh good!" she said as she clapped her hands together.

* * *

After what seemed like hours, Emily emerged from the hotel room, beaming as she twirled in the bright blue dress.

"Do you think he will like it Father?"

"I'm sure he will Emily. Are you ready to check out of the hotel now?"

"Yes," she said, still admiring how the dress flowed as she moved.

John went to fetch the trunk and his bag from the room. In the process of finding her dress, Emily had tossed a large part of his belongings on the floor. Sighing, he tossed them back in with little care. He would have a talk with her later. John put the bags on top the trunk and dragged it out to the desk. Emily was busy chatting with Nate, telling him her life story as if they were best friends.

"And when we get back to Seattle, Thomas and I will—"

"Excuse me," said John. "I hate to break up your conversation, but have you found us a wagon and driver yet?"

"One of the boys went up the street with a load a few minutes ago. I hollered at him and told him I had some passengers for him. He should be back by here pretty quick," said Nate.

"Fine," said John. "Let's settle up for the rooms."

John paid for the two rooms and reluctantly gave Nate a tip for arranging their transportation. He was no help whatsoever when Emily was missing and he seemed to be a lazy sort. John decided to keep him happy since he might need his services again soon.

"Thank you sir. Will you be staying here when you come back through?"

"More than likely," said John as he grabbed Emily's bag and dragged the rest of the luggage out the door and onto the street. "Thanks," he shouted over his shoulder as the door closed behind them.

The town had come alive in the last hour. People were hustling up and down the street, going about their business. Most were new arrivals, wide-eyed and clueless, on their way to make their fortune. John wondered how many would be successful, how many would return broke, and how many would never be seen again.

They didn't have to wait long before a wagon pulled up, driven by an older gentleman with a short beard and trimmed hair. He wasn't near as scruffy looking as Billy.

"You the folks headed for Stella's?"

"Yes sir, that's us," said John.

"Name's Jack."

John reached up and shook Jack's hand. "I'm John Palmer and this is my daughter Emily."

"Well, let's get you loaded up and we'll be on our way," said Jack.

While the driver loaded the trunk and bags into the

wagon, John helped Emily up into the seat and then climbed up.

"Ready, set?" said Jack as he plopped into his seat.

"I have been ready for weeks," exclaimed Emily.

Jack looked at her father for confirmation. John nodded and the driver slapped the reins against the team of two horses. They were off.

* * *

The route to Stella's led them out of town, then along the banks of the Lowe River. It was a beautiful day with sun high in the northern sky. Emily marveled at how early the sun rose and how late at night it remained. With every passing day the hours grew longer. *Soon I will be able to read a book at midnight,* she thought.

The driver wasn't the talkative sort. John asked him about the history of the area but had to pry nearly every answer from him—until he asked about the wildlife.

"We had a fair number of moose around, but they've been hunted pretty hard by the market hunters," said Jack.

"Market hunters?" asked Emily.

"They hunt for moose, sheep, and black bear and sell the meat in town," said Jack. "Bringing in beef is awful expensive."

Emily wasn't sure she liked the idea of market hunting, even though she now realized Thomas was doing the same. "Won't they wipe out all the animals?" she asked.

"Maybe," said Jack. "I expect it's going to be harder and harder to find the critters. The hunters already are having to travel further to find game."

"Well, I don't think I like market hunting," she said.

"Man's gotta eat," said Jack matter-of-factly.

"What about bears?" asked John. "Are there many around here?"

"There are a lot of them about, both black bear and grizzly. When the salmon are running they congregate along the river and can be trouble."

"Do you see many along this road?" asked Emily nervously.

"Sometimes. Most of the time they just run away, but I did have a big grizzly charge the team last week."

"What happened?" said Emily, her face turning pale.

"Ah, it was just a false charge. The bear stopped about fifteen feet away and then ran off. Horses didn't care for it though."

John could see this was troubling Emily. He decided to try and change the subject. "How much further?"

"Another mile or two. Shouldn't be too much longer."

With that, silence fell on the group. Emily spent her time looking at the high mountains lining both sides of the valley. She had never experienced scenery like this and she wanted to take it all in. The upper reaches of the mountains were still brown, but spring was slowly invading, turning the drab into a multitude of shades of green. Plunging herself into the beauty of the surroundings helped pass the time, but she couldn't entirely calm her excitement about the reunion that was now so close.

John lit up his pipe for a smoke as they traveled along the winding, sometimes muddy trail. It was a primitive wagon road and the amount of traffic had left it deeply rutted in spots. Portions of the road stretched across jagged rocky patches, imperiling both the wagon and the horses. Occasionally they hit a bump that threatened to bounce Emily off the wagon but John was quick to anticipate and grab hold. Jack said nothing as they bounced along, apparently oblivious to the rough ride.

"About another half mile and we'll be there," Jack said, finally breaking his silence.

"Can you wait for us at her place until we see if she can put us up?" asked John.

"I can wait for a few minutes, but I got other work to do today."

"If Stella doesn't have room for us can you leave us there and then return in time to take us back to town before dark?"

"I suppose I can do that."

"And if we do stay, how can we arrange transportation back to town when we are ready to leave?"

"Best way is to pass a note to one of the travelers coming to town from north of the canyon. Get it to Nate at the hotel and he can find someone to come get you."

"Okay, thank you for the information. Sure can be hard arranging things around here being so remote."

"We do all right," said Jack.

* * *

The wagon rounded a bend in the road, and in the distance, the canyon came into clear view. Keystone Canyon was a narrow gorge through which the river flowed. Emily wondered if they had to travel through it or up and around. Either prospect frightened her as the water was swift and the walls steep. Just as she was about to ask, Jack spoke up.

"Almost there. Just around this next little corner is Stella's place."

As they passed a couple of small, dilapidated cabins along the trail, Emily's impending anxiety turned to anticipation at the news.

"Is Stella the only one that lives out here?" she asked.

"Nope. There are a few families living out this way, but the cabins are few and far apart."

"Why does she choose to live way out here?" asked Emily.

"Lots of folks traveling up the canyon and beyond so her husband decided it was a good place to build."

"Oh, she is married?"

"Nope, widowed. Went out hunting and never came back. Gone for four or five years, I think."

"That's terrible," said Emily. "Didn't anyone look for him?"

"Yep. A bunch of us spent a week or so looking for him, but we never found a sign. It's like the land just swallowed him up. Ah, here we are," said Jack.

They had rounded the corner and a tidy white house came into view. It was unlike the other buildings they had passed. Instead of a log cabin, this one was made from real lumber, rough cut from a sawmill. It almost looked out of place among the rustic buildings that dominated the area. They turned off the wagon road and Jack pulled the team up next to the front porch.

Emily was off the wagon with a single, unladylike bound and headed for the front door.

"Wait here," said John as he jumped off the wagon. "I'll be back in a moment to let you know if we need a ride back tonight."

"Okay," said Jack. "But don't be too long. I gotta get back."

"Emily, wait," John shouted.

She stopped just short of the stairs. John had wanted to counsel her before they got here but with the confusion of the morning and her little disappearing act he didn't have the opportunity.

"Emily, no matter what happens I want you to be calm."

"What do you mean?"

"Well, we don't know if Thomas is still here. Even though folks have seen him in town, there is no guarantee he hasn't moved on."

"But he is in business with Miss Stella. That's what Mr. Parker at the store told me."

"I know. I just want you to be prepared in case things don't go the way you expect."

"He's here. I just know it," she said as she started up the steps.

"Let me take the lead. And I will do the talking until we find out if he is here."

Emily sighed and relented, following her father up the steps to the front door.

A welcome sign hung on the door. John hesitated, not knowing if they should knock or just walk in. He decided to take the more conservative approach and knocked on the door.

"Coming," said a voice from inside the house.

The door opened and they were greeted by a trim woman in her fifties, with graying hair and blazing blue eyes.

"I'm Stella. May I help you?" she said, glancing past them at Jack waiting on the wagon.

"Hello, my name is John Palmer and this is my—"

"Is Thomas Thornton here?" Emily shouted from behind her father, unable to contain herself any longer.

"He's not here now but I expect him back today or tomorrow," said Stella. "My, don't tell me you are Emily, his young lady friend."

"Yes," said Emily. "Where is he? Is he alright?"

"He's doing fine. He went out on a hunting trip yesterday and said he would be gone two or three days."

"So he might be back tonight?" asked Emily hopefully.

"Perhaps. But I wouldn't worry if he isn't. He promised he would be gone no more than three days."

Emily was crestfallen. She had built herself up to this moment and now she might have to wait yet another day before she could see Thomas.

John turned his attention to the matter at hand. "Do you have room to put us up for the night? I need to let Jack know so he can get back to town."

"Of course," said Stella. "I have plenty of room right now. Come on in."

"I have to pay Jack first and fetch our luggage from the wagon."

"Emily, come on in dear and sit down while your father tends to business."

Stella took Emily under her wing and ushered her into the house as John headed down the stairs.

"I overheard what was going on," said Jack. "Guess you won't be needing me to come back tonight."

"No, we are set for tonight at least. What do I owe you?"

"Four bucks and we'll call it even," said Jack.

"I'll make it five if you help me get this luggage to the porch."

"Deal," said Jack as he jumped down from the seat.

They carried the trunk with the two bags on top to the porch. With the money in hand, Jack headed back to the wagon and leapt up into the seat.

"Thanks for all your help. I may call on you again,"

said John.

"You bet. Be happy to do business with you again," said Jack as he slapped the reins and the wagon headed off to town.

John left the trunk on the porch and carried the bags into the house. Emily was sitting in an overstuffed chair, leaning forward and listening intently as Stella told her about how Thomas had ended up in her care. John took a seat next to her.

"Has he told you about me?" asked Emily.

"He hasn't said much, but I can tell he misses you," said Stella.

That seemed to please Emily. She had so many worries, both about his health and whether he still cared for her.

"I can't believe you folks came all the way up here," said Stella.

"Emily couldn't wait for the mail for news so we decided to take a little adventure," said John.

"Thomas wrote you a letter. Didn't you get it?"

"No, it appears we left before it arrived," said John.

"What did it say?" asked Emily.

Stella smiled. "I didn't read it, dear. I know he was concerned about finding work and sorting out his plans."

"Sorting out his plans?" asked Emily. "What do you mean?"

"Well, I don't think he has really decided what to do next. He doesn't have enough money for the supplies needed to head into the Interior. I'm hoping he doesn't decide to venture out until he's properly outfitted."

"Well I'm sure once he sees we are here he will want to return to Seattle," said Emily.

Stella glanced at John to see his reaction but, couldn't

read him. While she wasn't sure of Thomas' plan, Stella was fairly certain a quick return to Seattle wasn't a part of it. He still had a pretty good case of gold fever and based on what Stella knew of him, returning without even trying would feel like failure.

"I'm not sure he will be ready to do that," said Stella gently. "I think he has his heart set on finding gold."

"But surely once he sees me he will change his mind. We can return to Seattle and be married. I'm sure he will want that."

John was about to say something when Stella intervened.

"You two look hungry after a bumpy wagon ride. Come on into the dining room and I'll fix you some lunch."

"We don't want to be any trouble," said John.

"No trouble at all. I've got a nice pot of moose stew on the stove and biscuits ready to go into the oven."

"Sounds good," said John as he stood and motioned for Emily to do the same.

"Some lunch will do you good, Emily," he said as he herded her off to the dining room.

Chapter 25

It took Thomas a long while to make his way back up the game trail to where he left the horse along the creek. Thankfully, she was still there and waiting for him. He secured the pack to the horse, removed the round from the chamber of the .45-70, and put it in the scabbard. Untying the horse, he headed off up the trail, leading her through the brush.

It was too late in the day to try and make it back home. Besides, he wasn't quite prepared to face Stella with the news he had to deliver. All he wanted to do at this point was make it back to camp, cook a hot meal, and get some rest.

They were about half way back to camp when the horse suddenly stopped, her ears up and refusing to move. Thomas tugged on the lead but she stood firm. She sensed something off the trail to the right. Thomas stopped and listened but heard nothing but the creek bubbling in the distance. Still it made him a bit nervous. He tugged again and the horse remained frozen in her tracks.

The grizzly exploded from the alders, making a nerve shattering woof and popping its jaws. Thomas instantly turned to yank the rifle from the scabbard but the horse spooked and whirled about, taking the gun out of reach. The bear stopped at thirty feet, swaying back and forth and still popping it's jaws, obviously agitated. He needed to get the .45-70 but the horse kept turning just enough to make it impossible to grab on the other side.

Thomas threw himself across the saddle on his stomach and grabbed the stock of the rifle, pulling it from the scabbard. As he slid to the ground, the bear let out another blood curdling growl and charged forward. Thomas had heard about false charges, but this didn't look like one and he wasn't about to find out. *I am not going to end up like Wesley,* he thought as raw adrenaline dumped into his veins. He racked the lever and raised the gun as the bear closed the distance to ten feet. Thomas fired. The shot further spooked the horse and she ran back down the trail. The bear staggered to one side, paused for a split second, and kept coming as Thomas racked another round. He fired just as the bear sideswiped him, knocking him to the ground and sending the .45-70 flying into the brush.

With the air nearly knocked out of him, Thomas rolled to his left and stood, turning to face the mauling he was sure to receive. Instead his ears were met with a chilling, piercing sound. It was the death cry of the grizzly. His second round had mortally wounded the bear as it shot past him. Now it lay dying in the brush, its life blood spilling out on the ground. Thomas looked frantically for the .45-70, finding it a few feet away and still in one piece. He racked another round and fired, putting the bear out of its misery. Dropping his arms to his side, he collapsed to the ground, shaking uncontrollably.

* * *

It took Thomas a while to collect himself. He stood up slowly, firmly clutching the .45-70 in his right hand as the shaking began to subside. He now found himself with a dead grizzly and a missing horse. Without Horse it would take him an impossibly long time to get home. Worse yet, all his gear was on the horse, along with Wesley's remains. *This is a fine mess,* he thought.

He had to find Horse; he would deal with the bear later.

He whistled loudly, hoping the horse was trained to respond to such a call. Listening intently, he hoped to hear hooves on the trail but only the sound of the creek reached his ears. He would have to search for her, hoping she hadn't strayed too far from the game trail. If she had, he may never find her.

He worked his way slowly along the game trail, stopping frequently to listen. His nerves were still frayed and his imagination placed a bear behind every tree. Fifteen minutes later he found Horse in a small meadow, nonchalantly eating grass. He approached carefully, not wanting to spook her. At his approach she looked up, turned towards him, and then continued eating. Thomas walked up slowly and grabbed the reins.

"You seem to be no worse for wear." The horse shook her head up and down and snorted as if in agreement.

Apparently the experience was not as traumatic for her as it was for him. Thomas checked to make sure nothing had been lost and to his relief, his pack and gear were still firmly lashed to the horse. He led her back up the game trail, making sure his grasp of the reins was firm. The horse seemed to tense a bit as they approached the bear kill, but Thomas patted her reassuringly. He stopped short of the bear and tied her off to an alder.

For a brief moment, Thomas thought about leaving the bear and heading back to camp. He didn't need a bear hide, though he could probably sell it in town. In the end his conscience won out.

It was a large boar, bigger than any bear he had ever seen. It was all he could do to roll it onto its back so he could remove the hide. He hit it both times during the charge, the first shot piercing it's lungs but not slowing it down. The second shot entered through the shoulder, breaking bone as the bear swept past him. Even mortally wounded, the bear had kept coming. It was a formidable beast.

It took him a little over and hour to skin the bear. He decided not to take the skull back with him. Instead he hung it in a tree as high as he could reach. Perhaps he would return for it someday. He removed some of the meat of the backstrap and placed it in an outer pouch of the pack. Using a bit of cord, he rolled the bear hide up and tied it securely. Straining to lift the hide, he was surprised at the weight of it. The horse didn't look too thrilled as Thomas heaved the hide up onto the pack frame and secured it. Once he added the camp gear, the horse was going to be heavily loaded for the trip home.

Although Thomas remained on high alert, the trip back to camp was uneventful. It was late afternoon when he removed the burden from the horse and tied her off so she could graze. Walking to the edge of the knoll in front of the tent, Thomas surveyed the valley below. He couldn't see the game trail or the spot where he killed the bear. He fetched his binoculars and returned, surveying the open areas in the valley far below. Within moments he spotted a small open area that caught his eye. The grass was disturbed, causing variation in color. Squinting through the binoculars it came into view—the cross he built. Wesley was in plain sight all along. He sat down and for a long time gazed at the valley and the meadow where life had been lost years before...

As the sun drifted low in the sky, Thomas built a roaring fire. He was famished and looked forward to having a hot meal. He took the backstrap from the pack and examined it. Most people wouldn't eat grizzly, preferring black bear if they ate bear meat at all. It smelled okay and since the bear wasn't near a supply of fresh fish, he reasoned it should be edible.

Thomas took the cast iron skillet Stella provided and set it near the fire on a crude stove top made of stones.

With the bear steak sizzling, a bit of sliced potato rounded out the menu. Thomas made sure it was good and done, then cut off a small chunk and tasted it hesitantly. It had a unique flavor but was entirely edible. Thomas ate heartily, enjoying every bit of the meal.

As the evening set in and the air began to cool, Thomas packed up as much of his gear as possible. *I need to get an early start in the morning.*

Tomorrow was going to be a long and difficult day, in more ways than one.

Chapter 26

After lunch, Emily spent the remainder of the day staring out the window, listening for the sound of the horse that would bring Thomas to her. Several times she thought she heard something and ran out to the porch, only to find it was some weary traveler heading out to seek their fortune. Disappointed, she would shrink back inside and take up her position at the window.

John had a long conversation with Stella about Valdez, the gold rush, and how she came to be there. She relayed how she and Wesley came to this new land and what grand dreams they had. Briefly she mentioned his disappearance and John didn't pursue it, seeing it was still a source of much emotion for her.

He marveled at her strength. Few women had what it took to thrive alone on the frontier.

I wonder how Lydia would handle this lifestyle, he thought, quickly thinking himself silly at the very notion of it. Stella stood up, interrupting his thoughts.

"My, I didn't realize how late it was getting. I need to get dinner started."

"Don't go out of your way for us," said John.

"It's no trouble, besides, I want to have something ready in case Thomas gets back tonight."

Emily turned from the window. "When will he ever get here," she said, pouting and sounding more like a spoiled child than a young lady.

"There is no guarantee he will return today Emily," said John.

"But he simply must."

"We have waited this long, one more night won't be much more difficult."

"But he could still get here tonight, couldn't he?"

"He might," said Stella. "But if he isn't here by the time the sun sets, I doubt he will show up. It really isn't safe for him to be traveling in the dark."

Emily clearly wasn't happy at the prospect of waiting another night.

John could tell she grew more restless with each passing moment. *Sometimes she is such a child.* He wondered if she was ready to be engaged, ready to be married and start a family.

He and Lydia started out young, perhaps too young. He didn't really know her well when they married. Her true personality emerged over the years, leading him to push down the feelings of regret that all too frequently overcame him. Emily was the only bright spot in their now stale marriage. After so many childless years she came along as he approached his thirtieth birthday.

The thought of losing her to Thomas saddened him, nearly as much as the prospect of abiding with Lydia alone. *Why couldn't Lydia be more like Stella?*, he thought, guilt immediately overtaking him. Though he knew it was wrong, he felt a strong attraction to this remarkable woman; self-sufficient, independent, yet compassionate and giving.

"Dinner," called Stella from the kitchen, saving John from his thoughts.

"I'm not hungry," said Emily, still staring out the window.

"You're going to eat," said John. "You don't want to be so weak you faint when you see Thomas," he said, smiling. He gently put his hands on her shoulders and steered her to the dining room.

"Oh, Father," she said, protesting feebly.

"Come on, sit down and let's eat," said Stella cheerfully. "He won't get here any faster if we starve ourselves."

Stella had prepared a hearty dinner with more food than three people could possibly eat. A nice roast, potatoes from last year's garden, and homemade bread.

"This pot roast is wonderful," said Emily.

"It's black bear," said Stella.

Emily paused in mid-bite, her eyes widening. "Bear?"

"Yes," said Stella, smiling.

John laughed out loud at his daughter's reaction. "Not quite the kind of food we have at home," he said, chuckling. "But it is marvelous, and you are a fantastic cook Stella."

"Thank you," said Stella.

Emily thought she saw Stella blush a bit but she wasn't sure. She also thought the way her father looked at Stella was a bit out of character but dismissed it as her imagination.

Conversation around dinner turned to the gold rush and how things had changed so much in the last few years because of it.

"How is your boarding house business doing?" asked John. "Are we the only ones here?"

"It has been slow lately. I was supposed to have a couple of miners stay the day before yesterday but they never showed up."

"How do you stay in business?"

"Well, Wesley and I did well in years past so I have enough to get by. And I still get a lot of business every time another gold find is announced."

"You've got a nice place here. I hope business picks up for you."

"Thank you, John. I'm sure it won't be long before the next stampede," she said, smiling.

Emily looked up from her half eaten chunk of bear. "Has Thomas said anything about going mining?"

"As far as I know he is still planning on it. He's just trying get enough money to buy supplies and equipment," said Stella.

"Well, I think he should come home with us," she said matter-of-factly. "With all that's happened I think it is best."

"I understand, but whether you know it or not, he is a strong-willed boy," said Stella. "I think you'll have a hard time convincing him to give up his dream. Besides, this country seems to suit him."

"I can convince him. Father, you can find him a job in Seattle, can't you?"

"I could," said John. "But do you think he would really be happy if you force him to give up his dream and settle down in Seattle?"

"I could make him happy," said Emily flatly.

"Perhaps, but not pursuing your dreams can leave you with life long regrets," said John, reflecting on his own experience. "What if he asks you to stay here with him?"

Emily looked down and poked at the food on her plate with her fork. She could feel the eyes of her father on her, waiting for a response. "I don't know."

"Well, it's something you should think about in case he asks. As I see it, you have two possible outcomes," said John. "Either he will ask you to stay or you will return home and wait for him, however long that may take."

"I don't think I like either of those choices," said Emily.

"I just want you to be prepared. I know all along you have assumed he will return with us," said John. "From what Stella has told us, I doubt that is likely."

"I'm finished," said Emily. Rising from the chair and brushing her hands to her side, she whisked around and returned to the window.

John found her behavior embarrassing. "I'm sorry," he whispered to Stella.

"Don't worry. I'm sure she will sort it out. She is, after all, totally out of her element."

"That's true. I just wish she would see the big picture."

"She'll be fine," said Stella. "I think she is stronger than you realize."

"I hope so," said John.

* * *

The evening passed slowly for Emily. Her father and Stella engaged in deep conversation, at times in lowered voices.

"His disappearance affected me greatly," said Stella, her voice lowered. "At times I didn't think I could go on without Wesley."

"It must have been hard for you," said John, leaning in so Emily couldn't hear. With Thomas still out, the conversation would have upset her.

Emily assumed they were talking about her, but cared little—her attention was focused elsewhere.

As the sun set, Emily's hope faded. The dim gray of night spread across her view.

"He isn't coming," she said.

"No, I'm sure he is camped out and probably already asleep," said Stella.

"I think I will stay up and wait in case he comes back in the middle of the night."

"Emily, he isn't coming back tonight. You need some rest, it has been a long day," said John.

Emily resisted but in the end her father won out. With thanks to Stella for her hospitality, John and Emily retired to their rooms.

As Emily lay in bed, fighting the sleep that was inevitable, she thought of Thomas, wherever he was. *Tomorrow will be the day*, she repeated to herself as she closed her eyes and sleep drifted over her.

Chapter 27

It rained all night, the wind adding its voice to the storm. Thomas had a fitful nights sleep. The storm only added to the anxiety he already suffered as he thought about facing Stella. Shortly before daybreak the rain ceased and the winds calmed. Thomas was now fully awake, forced to face the day with only a few hours of restless sleep.

He skipped making breakfast, instead eating some jerky and a dry biscuit. Though the storm was past, everything was wet, including the horse. She had little shelter from the storm. Thomas found her huddled up next to a small spruce tree where she apparently tried to escape the downpour.

Thomas fetched his blanket from the tent and used it to dry her off as much as possible. Fortunately he had the foresight to stash the saddle blanket in the tent overnight so she could start the day out dry.

He broke camp, shaking as much water as he could from the tent. It didn't take long for him to pack everything up and lash it all to the horse. She was pretty well loaded down by the time the bear hide was tied on, what with the wet gear and all. To make it worse, there was really no room for him to ride. It would take forever to make it back walking.

Thomas unloaded the bear hide and camping gear. Though he didn't like the idea of delaying his start, it was obvious he needed to do something. He fetched the axe and set about constructing a travois. Finding the needed poles was easy; the small stand of spruce on the knoll provided trees of the right size, and they were nice and straight. Even so it took him the better part of two hours to complete the pole sled.

So much for getting back this afternoon, he thought. It was mid-morning by the time everything was loaded up and the travois rigged so Horse could pull it. By then the sun was up, shining brightly in a clear blue sky. Thomas was glad for the warmth after the damp night, still the trail home would be muddy and slippery, making for slow going. He resigned himself to the fact it would be dinner time or later by the time he made it home. Once he reached the trail over the pass, he hoped he could ride, but that depended how much mud and water he encountered. He gave one last look down the valley at the meadow far below, turned, and led the horse up the trail.

* * *

John awoke with the sun streaming through the window of his room. He looked at his watch; seven-fifteen. He dressed and headed to the living area, only to find Emily in her chair, staring out the window. Stella was up and working on breakfast.

"She was there when I got up at six," said Stella, nodding towards her from the kitchen.

"Looks like it's going to be a long day," said John, smiling faintly. He walked over to the window.

"Emily dear, he isn't going to be here for a while. Stella told me it would probably take him six or more hours to make the trip back. No point in staring out the window all day."

"I have nothing better to do."

"Well, you could offer to help Stella do something around here. It would help pass the time."

"Perhaps," she said, dismissing the thought.

John went to the kitchen to find Stella frying potatoes

and homemade sausage. The coffee pot was idling on the back of the stove.

"Good morning John. Would you like some coffee?"

"You bet I would," he said, reaching for a cup. "I'll get it."

He poured a cup of coffee. It was black and strong, just the way he liked it. "Anything I can do to help?"

"Well since you asked, would you mind fetching some wood from the shed out back? I need to restock to keep my stove running," she said, smiling.

"Sure thing," said John, setting down his coffee and heading out the back door without hesitation.

He returned shortly, his arms piled high with wood. "Where do you want it?"

"Just drop it in the wood box there."

John felt a little silly for asking such an obvious question. The box was right next to the stove. He stacked the wood neatly and returned to his cup of coffee.

"Thank you John."

"You're welcome. It's the least I can do for you putting us up. Speaking of which, how much do we owe you for the rooms?"

"Nothing. You're my guests."

"Stella, I appreciate that, but we didn't come here to impose. Please, let me pay you."

"No, you are here for Thomas and that makes you my guests. I don't want to hear anymore about it," she said, feigning irritation.

John realized he wasn't going to win the argument so he relented. "I can't thank you enough."

"Well, I may still put you to work around here if you stay a while," she said, smiling.

Stella dished up breakfast and carried three plates to

the table in one swift move. "Breakfast's on. Come and eat, Emily."

Emily didn't resist. She was a bit hungry after picking through dinner the night before. John was already seated by the time she got to the table. She sat and looked at her plate. It looked appetizing, sausage and potatoes with a side of homemade toast and jam. Yet she was suspicious.

"More bear?" she asked.

John shot a quick glance at her and she understood his message immediately.

"No dear," said Stella. "It's moose breakfast sausage. My own special recipe."

"You made it yourself?" asked Emily.

"Yes, it's quite simple really. And it tastes wonderful if I do say so myself. Please try it."

Emily sliced off a small bite and tasted it. Stella was right; it was wonderful. She dug in and ate more like a hungry logger than a young lady. Her father watched, somewhat amazed at the way she consumed her breakfast.

"You must be very hungry," he said.

"I am, and this is the best breakfast I've had on the whole trip."

"Me too," said John as he winked at Stella.

"Thank you, but it's really just a simple meal," said Stella. "It's all this fresh air and adventure that's made you hungry," she said, smiling.

"May I help you clean up?" Emily said as they finished eating.

"Oh, you don't have to do that."

"I insist Miss Stella. You've been on your feet all morning."

"Okay, but I'll help you fetch the water and get it heating for the dishes."

"I'll get the water," said John. "You can give Emily a lesson in the intricacies of cooking on a wood stove."

The well was in a room near the back porch, a necessary precaution to keep it from freezing in the winter months. The old pump squeaked with each stroke as he filled the large pot with ice cold water. *I'm glad her attitude has improved,* thought John as he worked the pump.

He returned with the pot and put it on the stove. Stella was explaining to Emily how a wood fired cooking stove worked, how to stoke it, and proper operation of the damper.

"Everything under control?" asked John.

"Oh yes," said Stella. "I'll have her up to her elbows in dirty dishes in no time."

Emily smiled and turned back to scraping the plates.

"What is the soonest Thomas could return?" asked John.

"I doubt he will be back before three this afternoon," said Stella, "Assuming he left first thing this morning."

"I need to send a telegram to my wife. Do you think the lines are up now?"

"I know the crews have been working hard on getting the poles replaced and the lines back up, but I haven't heard if they're done with the repairs," said Stella.

"If I can I'd like to hitch a ride into town and see. Maybe I can write a message and have the operator send it when he is able," said John. "Would it be alright if Emily stayed here with you? I'm sure I couldn't drag her away from here today."

"Of course she can stay. We can think up a special welcome back meal for Thomas," said Stella.

Emily looked up from her work and nodded approvingly. "You're right Father, I'm not leaving here today for any reason."

"Well it's settled then. I'll hang out by the trail and see if I can't hitch a ride into town. We really need to get a message to your mother and let her know we are fine."

"How will you get back?" asked Emily.

"I'm sure I can arrange for a ride back. I'll check in with Nate at the hotel and tell him I'm going to need transportation. After all, I left him a big tip last time so he should be amenable," said John, smiling. "And I plan to be back before three for sure."

"Maybe you should wait until Thomas returns so we can let mother know we found him."

"No, its been long enough for her to wait for word. We'll send another telegram once we talk to Thomas and sort out our plans."

John scooped up his hat and coat and headed for the door. "I'll see you two ladies this afternoon," he said as he stepped out onto the porch. They called goodbye as he walked down the stairs, hiking briskly towards the wagon trail.

* * *

It only took two refills of his pipe for John to catch a ride with an outfitter headed into Valdez. He had little news from up the trail, but was pretty sure the telegraph lines were repaired. This gave John hope he would be able to send a message to Lydia and hopefully get a response the next day.

The driver dropped him off at the hotel, where John made arrangements for transport out of town just after noon. Leaving the hotel, he walked up the street until he found the telegraph office. It was open, which John hoped was a sign he would be able to send his message.

As soon as he entered the office, John heard the clattering of a telegraph key. The office was staffed by an operator seated in the corner and a clerk standing behind the counter. The operator seemed to be working furiously at the key while the young man at the counter sorted and stacked incoming messages.

"Can I help you?" said the clerk.

"Yes, I'd like to send a telegram to Seattle. Is that possible?"

"Yes sir. We just got the lines back up yesterday afternoon. We've been working like mad catching up with all the backlogged messages that are coming in."

"If you are that busy, when would my message go out?"

"Things will slow down towards evening. We should be able to get it out tonight," said the clerk . The operator nodded his concurrence as he continued to transcribe incoming Morse code.

"That will be fine," said John.

"Just fill out your name, information, and the message," said the clerk as he handed John a yellow form.

John kept the message brief, telling Lydia they had arrived, were safe, and waiting for Thomas to return from a short trip. He added they would contact her again once their plans were firmed up. He signed the message simply "John" and handed the form back to the clerk.

"Okay sir, let me just count up your words here." He quickly counted the words in the message and then announced, "That'll be four bits Mr. Uh... Palmer."

As John dug in his pocket for the change, the operator signaled a hold to the incoming message and said, "John Palmer?"

"Yes, how did you know?"

"We got a message in for you a few hours ago. It's somewhere in the stack there."

The clerk proceeded to flip back and forth through the pile of messages until he found it. He looked at it to confirm and then turned a bit pale. Handing it to John he said, "I think you should sit down before you read it, sir."

John gave him a puzzled look as he reached for the telegram. It was from Preston.

```
TO: JOHN PALMER, VALDEZ ALASKA
FROM: PRESTON VAN SANT, SEATTLE

Fire caused by faulty kerosene lamp.
House and out buildings total loss.
Lydia did not survive. Buried four
days ago.

With deepest regrets.

-- Preston --
```

John slumped to the chair, the telegram falling from his hand to the floor. He picked it up and stared at it again, not believing what he read. The realization came over him; everything was lost. His marriage was not the best, but he never would have left her, never would have wished such an ending. He fought back his grief.

"I'm sorry sir," said the clerk. "Can I do anything for you?"

John looked down for a long moment and finally said, "Not unless you can tell me how to break this news to my daughter."

"I'm truly sorry sir. Do you still want to send your message?"

"No, tear it up," said John as he stuffed the telegram in his pocket and left the office.

* * *

Thomas reached the low pass separating him from Goat Creek. He paused and looked at his pocket watch. *Nearly one-thirty.* Traveling up the wet and muddy trail to the saddle had slowed his progress, taking nearly twice as long as he anticipated. He checked the travois to make sure it was holding up to the abuse of the trail. Hopefully in another quarter mile the trail would flatten out enough for him to ride.

As he descended the saddle through the shale into Goat Creek, Thomas caught something out of the corner of his eye. It was a small band of Dall sheep, feeding down the slope just a few hundred yards ahead of him. This was an opportunity he couldn't pass up. He quickly determined there was enough time to take a sheep, field dress it, and still get back before dark—if he hurried. He waited until the sheep fed their way into a small draw out of sight, then stashed the horse out of view and started his stalk.

The wind was in his favor, blowing up the valley at a gentle pace. Thomas slowly worked his way down the slope, and up the backside of the small draw. Near the top, he got down low and crawled the rest of the way.

Peering over the edge, he saw two good sized rams along with a number of ewes. As near as he could tell, they were a mere sixty yards from him, well within range of the .45-70. He eased the gun up in place, rested it on a small boulder, and took aim. He placed the sights on the largest ram and slowly began to squeeze the trigger.

Before the gun could fire, a ram that lagged behind the group came into plain view just ten yards from him and spooked. This set the whole group on high alert and they turned and ran full tilt up the side of the draw, headed for the top of the mountain.

They were at eighty yards now, quartering away and moving fast. Thomas stood and whistled with no effect. He raised the gun, and drawing on his duck hunting experience on the farm, picked out the large ram and aimed a foot or so in front of it and pulled the trigger. The ram went head over heels and rolled out of sight as the bullet struck home. The rest of the group didn't slow to see what happened, but ran even faster and were soon topping the next ridge. Thomas was pretty sure the ram was down the way it toppled, but he approached cautiously just in case there was enough life in it to make a run for it.

Just over the top of the far side of the draw he found the ram. Though he led it a fair distance, the bullet struck the spine just ahead of the rear quarters. The sheep was down, its back broken, but it was still alive. As Thomas approached, it pawed the ground with its front feet in a desperate attempt to escape. Thomas dispatched it with a single shot just behind the ear.

After the moose incident, he had sworn he wouldn't wound an animal again and yet he had. *I have to learn to control myself*, he thought. He needed the money but his respect for the wild game he hunted made him extremely unhappy with his performance. It hadn't suffered long, but that was little consolation.

The ram fell only a hundred yards or so from the trail. Thomas would be able to get the horse pretty close. This was good; he could field dress the ram and drag it to the horse without having to quarter it in the field.

Thomas fetched the horse and brought it down the trail as close to the kill as possible, without making her have to climb up the draw. He tied her off and retrieved the axe from the pack, then climbed back up to the ram.

Pulling his knife from the sheath, he set about the

task of field dressing the sheep. With the axe he split the rib cage, working as quickly as he dared. *The last thing I need is to cut myself*, he thought.

The ram was smaller than a moose of course, and he was glad for that. As he worked, the thought of a bear sneaking up from behind kept nagging at him. He knew it was unlikely, but with the events of yesterday still fresh in his mind, he kept a close eye out, pausing from his work frequently to look around.

Once it was dressed out, Thomas assumed he could drag the sheep downhill to the horse. This turned out to be more difficult than he had imagined. Even with the sheep field dressed, it still proved to be quite heavy and awkward to handle. Thomas worked the sheep downhill in short bursts of energy. By the time he got to the horse, sweat was pouring off him. He paused and took a long drink of water from his canteen, then set about rearranging the load on the travois to accommodate the sheep.

Fortunately, he had constructed the travois using fairly stout spruce poles and it was strong enough to bear the load of the sheep along with the grizzly hide and his other gear. Thomas secured everything, checked the pole attachments to the horse to ensure they were secure and not rubbing her, and mounted up. Another hour and a half slipped by. As he eased the horse slowly down the valley, he cringed at what Stella would do if he didn't make it back before dark.

* * *

For John, it was a long wagon ride back to the boarding house. He was lost in thought, even though the driver attempted to engage him in conversation.

"So you a miner?"

"No," said John.

"Most people coming through are miners. You going to do some logging? You look like you could be a logger, or maybe a fisherman?"

"Neither."

"You sure aren't much for conversation."

John stared at him as they bumped over the trail. "Look, I just received very bad news from home. I don't feel much like talking if you don't mind."

"What kind of news?" asked the driver.

What kind of clueless people inhabit this place? thought John, furrowing his brow into a glare.

"My wife is dead," said John flatly, staring straight into the drivers eyes.

"Oh. I see," said the driver.

Those were his last words. He stared straight ahead and refrained from looking at John, still feeling the heat of his glare.

John was thankful for the silence; his thoughts were in turmoil. He faced a great dilemma. Here Emily was expecting to see Thomas at any moment, and yet he had such terrible news to deliver. Should he wait? Not tell her at all? He didn't know what to do.

She had to be told, and yet he didn't want to take away the joy of her reunion with Thomas. He decided to wait. Perhaps not even tell her for a day or so. It made little difference really. Lydia was gone and buried, their house and property a total loss. All that remained of their life in Seattle was money in a bank and the burned out remnants of what was once a home. It didn't matter if Emily knew today, tomorrow, or next week.

The driver pulled up in front of the boarding house and stopped. John had been so lost in thought he hadn't realized they were so close. He stepped down from the wagon and paid the driver. By the time he had turned from the wagon, Emily was rushing down the steps toward him.

"When I heard the wagon I thought it was Thomas," she said.

"No, just me," said John quietly.

"Father, are you alright? You don't look well."

"I'm fine. Just a little tired from my trip this morning," he said, smiling weakly as he headed to the house.

Stella met them at the door. "Have you had lunch John?"

"No, but I'm not really hungry."

Stella could see something was wrong, but hesitated to pry. "Are you ill?" she asked.

"He's just tired from this trip," said Emily before her father could answer.

"I see. Well let me fix you a little something anyway. Come in and sit in the dining room."

John made his way into the house and took up a chair at the table in the dining room. Emily returned to her post next to the window in the other room.

"You really don't need to trouble yourself Stella. I can wait until dinner."

"It isn't any trouble," she said. "How about breakfast for lunch?" she asked cheerily. "I've got eggs and some potatoes I can fry up."

"That does sound good," said John.

Stella set about cooking while John sat quietly at the table.

"I forgot to ask. Did you send the telegram Father?" called Emily from her post.

John hadn't anticipated the question, although he should have realized it would come up. He reached into his pocket and clutched the crumpled telegram. "Yes dear, I wrote out a telegram to your mother," he said, telling a half-truth.

"Oh good," said Emily as she turned back to the window to continue her vigil.

John hadn't shed any tears, but knew he would when the time came. Telling Emily would bring them out, no matter how hard he fought to hold them back. He felt lost, homeless, and without direction in his life for the first time in many, many years. It dawned on him, *I am homeless. I have no where to go.* He had some serious decisions to make and yet he felt numb, not caring to think about the future.

"Here you go, John," said Stella as she set a heaping plate of eggs and potatoes before him.

"Thank you, but I don't think I can eat all this."

"That's fine," she said, smiling. "Just do the best you can."

"I'll try."

"Are you sure you feel okay? You don't look well," she said, lowering her voice so Emily wouldn't hear.

John looked at Stella and hesitated. She waited, expecting him to say something, and yet all he did was stare. As she was about to look away, he reached into his pocket and pulled out a crumpled piece of paper. He put it on the table, smoothed it out flat with both hands, then slid it over to her. As she reached for it he raised a single index finger to his lips and nodded in Emily's direction.

Stella picked up the paper. It was a telegram. As she read it, the color drained from her face. She put it down and reached across the table, placing her hand on John's. "I'm so sorry," she said, mouthing the words.

The warmth of her hand on his brought him an unexpected feeling of comfort. He had known her only a day but he could see she was a compassionate and caring woman. That much was evident in the way she had cared for Thomas.

"Thank you," he said as he pulled his hand back slowly, blinking back the tears while picking up the telegram and putting it in his pocket. In but a whisper he said, "I don't think I am going to tell Emily until Thomas returns safely. Perhaps tomorrow."

"I think that's wise," said Stella. "Is there anything I can do?"

"Well, I think we might need to stay a few days longer if that's okay with you."

"Of course it is John. You and Emily can stay as long as you like."

"Thank you," he said as he picked up his fork and began to eat. His appetite had returned.

* * *

Thomas made better progress down the valley than anticipated. He had to stop several times to check the load and make adjustments. The horse only slipped once on a particularly steep and slippery section of the trail. At first Thomas thought they were going down, but Horse recovered and regained her balance. It wasn't long until they made it through the spruce wall and were on the flat ground of the river bed. Here he made better progress towards home.

As he rode along, his thoughts turned to how he would tell Stella about his find on the mountain. Had he done the right thing by deciding to bring Wesley back? There was no way of telling for sure. He hoped she would take his word about what he found and not want to see the remains. Doubt crept into his mind. Perhaps he should have buried him beneath the crude cross of alder. The story would have to be carefully unfolded to gauge Stella's feelings. Only then would he know what he should reveal.

By the time he reached the wagon trail it was approaching dinner time. It would be another hour before he made the boarding house, but at least it would still be daylight.

He could imagine Stella standing at the window, waiting to chastise him if he was late. He stopped to water the horse and let her feed. He had pushed her hard and she deserved a bit of rest, even if only for a few minutes. Thomas fetched a carrot from his pack and gave it to Horse. She munched it down quickly and seemed to give him an appreciative look, even though it was Stella who packed the treat. He took a swig from the canteen and gnawed on a piece of jerky, then mounted up and pressed on.

He needed a plan. He would delay telling her about Wesley until he had taken care of his gear, skinned, quartered, and hung the sheep, and salted down the bear hide. Of course she would insist he eat first, so by the time that was over with and the rest of the chore completed it would be late. No, he wouldn't tell her tonight. He would wait until morning. It was then he realized the bear skull and Wesley's rifle were in plain sight, lashed to his pack. He stopped again, dismounted, and removed the rifle and bear skull. He wanted to hide them from view. Stella would probably want to see the bear hide unrolled so that wasn't an option.

There really was only one choice. Thomas untied the nearly dry tent and blankets from the travois and spread them on the ground. Placing the skull in the center and the Winchester next to it, he folded the ends in, then rolled it up and secured it with a cord. This concealed the contents well; you couldn't tell there was something hidden inside. Thomas placed the bundle back on the travois and tied it down. Now he was prepared for his arrival, but the sense of dread over what was to come weighed heavily upon him.

* * *

"Dinner," called Stella from the kitchen. "I've made a nice moose stew and fresh baked bread."

"Shouldn't we wait for Thomas?" asked Emily.

"We don't know what time he is coming dear. Let's eat and I'll keep some warm for him."

"But what if he doesn't come at all?"

"He gave me his word he would be back no later than tonight. Come, sit and eat."

John was already seated at the table when Emily pulled up a chair across from him and sat down.

"Do you think he's coming Father?"

"Yes, Emily. I'm sure he will be here soon," said John, hoping Thomas was alright. There would be enough heartbreak for his daughter soon enough without adding to it.

Stella brought plates and set the table, then returned with a pot of stew and a cutting board with a golden brown loaf of fresh bread. The smell made both John and Emily realize how hungry they were. Stella dished up the stew for each of them, then took her place at the table.

"Well, dig in," she said.

Emily was glad the stew wasn't made from bear meat. At least she thought she was. Eating moose sounded much more appetizing the eating bear. She tasted it carefully and found it delicious. As they ate, the conversation focused on Thomas.

"You never did tell us who shot him," said Emily.

"We don't really know. There are rumors but no one knows for sure," said Stella.

"Is there no way to find out? Someone should pay for what they did to him."

"It sounds to me like it would be very difficult to prove," said John. "Besides, from what Stella said, Thomas has moved on and is looking forward not backward."

"True," said Stella. "But if he ever did find out it would be hard to stop him from seeing justice served."

"My bet is he is focused more on his dream than on vengeance," said John.

"You're probably right," said Stella. "We can always ask him when he gets here," she said, smiling.

"And when will that be?" asked Emily, glancing back at her window for any sign of Thomas.

"Patience my dear, patience," said John. "This is a good life lesson for you."

"I have been patient Father. Now I'm ready for him to arrive," she said as she started to stand.

"Where are you going young lady?" said Stella. "Now sit down, I baked a nice cake for desert."

Emily slipped back into her chair obediently. John could tell she really didn't want cake. He gave her the look that told her to stay seated.

Stella went to the kitchen and returned with a lovely cake and three plates. As she pulled her chair out to sit down, they heard a noise come from the back of the house.

"What was that?" asked Emily.

"Could be a bear or some other critter. You stay here and I'll check," said Stella.

"Wait, I'll go with you," said John. "Wait here, Emily."

"Yes, Father," she said, stiffening in her chair and staring towards the back door.

They moved through the kitchen, past the pump room, reaching the back door. With Stella behind him, John slowly opened the door, hoping he wouldn't be face to face with a bear. What he saw was a horse next to the barn and a figure in the shadows untying something. Thomas had returned.

* * *

Stella breathed a sigh of relief. "Go back to Emily and I will bring him in and surprise the both of them," said Stella, smiling.

"Okay," said John as he turned and headed for the dining room.

"What was it?" asked Emily.

"Oh nothing. Must have been a bird or a squirrel," said John, telling a white lie and laboring to keep a straight face.

"Where's Stella?"

"She'll be back in a minute. She said she needed to fetch something from the barn."

Stella stepped out the back door and walked to the barn.

"Finally you're back," she said.

"Well," said Thomas solemnly, "I made it out with only a bit of excitement."

"I can see that," said Stella, eyeing the grizzly hide and the sheep. "Looks like you have some work ahead of you."

"Yes, I have to get this hide salted and the sheep skinned and quartered."

"Come in for a moment, I have a surprise for you."

"I really need to get this done first."

"This won't take long. Please, humor me," she said.

Thomas knew it was pointless to resist and followed Stella in through the back door. She slipped beside him and guided him by the shoulders towards the dining room. *This is odd*, he thought.

As they rounded the corner from the kitchen she said with a whisper, "We have visitors."

Thomas stopped short, trying to register what he was seeing. There sat Emily and her father, unaware of his approach. Thomas shot a questioning glance at Stella, but before he could say anything, Emily looked up from the table.

"Thomas!" she nearly screamed as she jumped up and rushed around the table towards him, her arms outstretched.

"Emily, what in the world are you—"

"We came to find you," she said as she wrapped her arms tightly around him.

"Emily, I'm all dirty and covered in blood."

"I don't care, I don't care" she said, tears streaming down her face.

He put his arms around her and hugged her, then looked over at John.

"Sir, what are you two doing here?"

"Emily insisted," said John. "You know how she is when she gets something in her mind."

"I was going to send a telegram to you as soon as the lines were repaired," said Thomas as he looked down at Emily.

"They are fixed now," she said. "Father sent a telegram to Mother today telling her everything was fine."

"Well I'm glad to see you, but am certainly surprised," said Thomas. "I can't imagine you made such a journey."

With that, Emily led Thomas by the hand to the table where they sat and she began to relay the events of the last several weeks. How she received the letter from Stella, begged her parents to come, the seasickness, running aground, and the foul weather they encountered.

Thomas listened intently to every word, looking at John now and then to gauge his thoughts on the whole experience.

"What happened to your forehead?" said Thomas, as he gently brushed her hair back, revealing a small cut.

She smiled. "Oh nothing, just the result of being slammed to the floor when we shipwrecked."

"I wouldn't call it a shipwreck," said John. "Just a minor grounding."

"Well I'm glad you made it here safely," said Thomas.

Stella brought Thomas a plate of food and he ate ravenously while Emily continued with the tale of their voyage. John sat quietly, rarely speaking. Thomas thought this out of character for the man that had always been friendly and outgoing towards him.

"And then we finally got here yesterday and I've been looking out that window waiting for you ever since," said Emily, completing the saga.

"Well," said Thomas. "I still can't believe you're here."

"Tell us what happened when you were shot," said

Emily.

"There isn't much to tell. I was walking down the street, someone called out, and the next thing I knew I was face down on the ground."

"Does it hurt much?" asked Emily.

"Not now. I had a very good nurse," he said, smiling at Stella.

Thomas finished his meal and stood up. "I don't want to be rude, but I really must take care of the horse and the game I brought back."

"I'll come and watch," said Emily as she jumped up from the table.

"I'll lend you a hand as well," said John.

Thomas first took care of the horse, removing the pack frame and the travois. He was careful to take the rolled tent from the pole sled and casually put it out of sight. He took his pack and did the same with it. He wasn't ready for any questions or accidental discoveries, especially in light of the current turn of events.

John helped him skin the sheep and quarter it, mainly by pulling the skin and holding on as Thomas directed. When the job was done, they hung the meat to age. Emily stood back, acting squeamish about the whole process. With the sheep hanging, Thomas turned his attention to the bear. He unrolled the hide and spread it out on the floor of the barn. It looked even larger now than when he had shot it.

"Let's measure it," said Thomas.

Thomas enlisted John to help him measure the bear. From tip of its nose to tail it measured nine and a half feet.

"Incredible," said John. "Were you scared when you shot it?"

Thomas explained how he wasn't hunting for bear, didn't want to shoot a bear, and tried to avoid them.

"But this one was looking for a fight and charged me at close range. Took me three shots to finish it and it knocked me down in the process."

"Amazing," said John as he looked over at Emily.

She was standing there, eyes wide, mouth agape.

"Thomas, you can't go back out in those woods. It's too dangerous."

Thomas just looked at her and said seriously, "Don't worry, I won this time."

This did little to comfort her. She was about to further argue her point when Stella came out from the house to check up on things.

"How big was the bear, Thomas?" she asked.

"Nine and half feet," he said.

"That's a mighty fine bear. Wesley shot one that big once. What are you going to do with it?"

"I'm going to flesh it out, salt it down, and see if I can't sell it to Noel down at the store. Maybe one of the tourists that pass through on the steamers will want to make a rug out of it."

Thomas decided the bear hide could wait until tomorrow. He was tired and more interested in hearing from Emily and her father than spending half the night scraping a hide. He took care of the rest of his things and unloaded the .45-70.

"I'm done for the night," he said. "The rest can wait till morning. Let's go in."

Emily and Thomas moved to the living room and sat next to each other on the bench by the window.

"I'm tired," said John. "I think I'll turn in."

Stella was certain the stress of holding the secret about

his wife had worn him down more than anything.

"Good night," said Stella as she continued with some cleanup in the kitchen. "I'm getting things set up for tomorrow, then I'll be ready to call it a day."

"Good night, Father."

"Have a good night sir," said Thomas.

"Goodnight you two. Now don't sit up all night talking," said John as he retired to his room.

"I'm worried about him," said Emily. "He hasn't looked well all day."

"He's probably just tired from the trip and all," said Thomas.

"I hope that's all it is."

A few moments later, Stella came from the kitchen. "Well, I've got everything cleaned up and ready to start another day tomorrow. Good night."

Stella turned in, leaving Thomas and Emily alone in the living room.

* * *

"Finally we can talk," she said. "I'm so glad you are okay."

"I'm doing fine. I'm sorry I didn't get word to you sooner."

"It doesn't matter. I had to come and see you, to find out if you were really okay."

"I'm glad to see you, but I still can't believe your mother let you make such a trip."

"Father had to convince her."

"Well I'm glad he did."

Her smile changed, as did her expression. Thomas wondered what was coming next.

"Thomas, I want you to come back to Seattle with me. Father has contacts, he can find you a good job and we can be married."

Thomas hadn't expected to face this issue so soon. He thought he had a year or more to make his fortune, then decide what to do—return to Seattle and Emily or stay in Alaska. She caught him off guard.

"Emily, you know I—"

"You must come back with me. This place is too dangerous and I don't want to lose you. I can't bear going months at a time wondering if you are alive or dead."

"Emily, we agreed on this before I left. I would spend a year to strike gold."

"Things have changed," she said flatly. "You've been shot, you have no money or supplies, this place is nothing like you or I imagined."

"Reality is always different than the dream, but that doesn't make the dream any less important," said Thomas.

"You care more about your dream than me?"

How do I answer that? thought Thomas.

"If you truly cared about my feelings there would be no argument. You would return with me."

"You know I care for you. But you have to see it from my point of view. If I don't do this I will regret it all my life."

Slowly Emily began to understand. This was something Thomas *had* to do. Something that would nag at him all his life if he didn't. And if she was the reason he gave up his dream, he would resent her as well. She could try to force her will on him but what kind of life would they have together? Perhaps none. She took his hand in hers.

"Thomas, I want you to be happy. If this makes you

happy then I understand. Let's make the most of the time we have together."

Thomas breathed a silent sigh of relief. "How long can you stay?"

"I don't know. Father has left our return open. We didn't know what we would find when we arrived."

"Well, perhaps you can stay for a while."

"At least until Mother demands we return," she said, laughing. "We'll see what she says in response to Father's telegram."

Their conversation turned to how Thomas planned to work until he earned enough money to move on to the gold fields. Emily listened intently as he described with enthusiasm the huge finds that were being made. His passion was evident, it even instilled in her a small bit of his excitement. As the evening wore on, she began to feel the effects of too little sleep and yawned.

"I can see I've carried on long enough," said Thomas, smiling.

"I'm sorry. I went to bed late and got up before anyone else so I could watch for you."

"Well then, I think it's time to turn in. I have a lot of work ahead of me and a chore I'm not looking forward to."

"What's that?" she asked.

"Oh, don't worry about it. I'll tell you tomorrow."

Thomas leaned forward, kissed her on the forehead, and said good night. He headed upstairs, pausing on the landing to watch Emily close the door to her room below.

I wish it was a chore rather than what I have to tell Stella, he thought as he closed the door to his room. Tomorrow would be tough.

Chapter 28

Morning came all too soon, at least for those in the boarding house carrying the burden of bad news.

Stella put on an amazing breakfast, complete with sausage, biscuits and gravy, and eggs. Conversation around the table was light, Emily showing her delight as she sat close to Thomas, hanging on his every word.

Shortly afterwards, John called to his daughter in the living room. "Emily, come, sit down at the table, I have some news from home."

Emily sat down next to him, tilting her head with a puzzled look. "But how? You just sent the telegram yesterday."

"There was a telegram waiting for me when I got to the office."

"From who?" she asked. "Mother?"

Stella moved close to Thomas and put her hand on his shoulder. He could see John was stressed. He wondered what sort of news he had to share; whatever it was, it didn't appear to be good.

"It was from Preston," said John as he moved closer to Emily and took both her hands in his.

"Emily, there was an accident."

"Is it Mother? Is she alright?" said Emily, nervously.

"Emily, there was a fire. Your mother didn't make it out."

Emily looked confused, as if what her father was saying didn't sink in. "What are you saying?" she said, her eyes reddening.

John paused. "Emily, your mother died in the fire." How horrible those blunt words sounded in his ears.

"No, it can't be!" said Emily, tears welling up in her

eyes. "You're wrong, there must be some mistake."

Thomas was shocked. He moved his chair next to Emily's and put his arm around her as she began to sob.

"There was a fire. They think it started from a faulty kerosene lamp. Everything was destroyed, the house, workshop, and all the out buildings," said John, his voice quivering.

The harsh reality set in; Emily broke down, crying uncontrollably. Thomas tried to comfort her but he understood this kind of sorrow meant tears would be shed. He put his hand on John's shoulder.

"I'm so, so sorry," said Thomas.

"We should never have come," said Emily, blurting out the words between her sobs. "Mother would still be alive."

"Or we all may have perished in the fire," said John. "Emily, we can't blame ourselves for this."

"We must go home," she said. "Mother would want us to be there."

John paused, afraid to tell her. "Emily, it's too late. She was buried five days ago. Since there was no way to get in touch with us, Preston had to take care of things."

"I didn't even get to say goodbye," said Emily, gasping to get the words out.

John fell silent, tears streaming down his cheeks. There were no words to comfort her.

"Here dear, have some tea," said Stella, returning from the kitchen with a tray. "It will make you feel better."

"Nothing will make me feel better ever," she said.

Thomas was at a loss for words. This turn of events made his task all the more difficult and untimely. *Should I wait to tell Stella?*

"Come dear, try the tea," said Stella. "I know how

you feel. I have felt the loss."

"I never thought about it that way," said Emily, trying in vain to dry her tears. "It is terrible to lose someone you love, but I suppose not knowing what happened to them makes it all the more painful."

"I know what happened to Wesley," said Thomas softly. All eyes were on him. Stella's face bore an expression of mixed shock and anticipation. "How do you know?"

"I found him beyond Goat Creek," said Thomas hesitantly.

"How do you know it's him?" Stella demanded.

Thomas reached into his pocket, and taking the watch, gave it to Stella, his hands closing over hers and remaining for a moment.

Stella opened her hands, slowly turning the watch over. As she read the inscription, a tear began to run down her cheek. "It's his," she said in a whisper. She sunk slowly into a chair. "Thomas, tell me what happened."

"I had made my way over Goat Creek and into the next valley where I camped the first night. The next morning I decided to explore down the creek. I was busting through brush when I came into a clearing and something caught my eye."

"What was it?," asked Emily.

"I moved closer and saw it was a bear skull, a very large one. I began to look around and found the watch and what remained of Wesley. It looks like he was attacked by the bear, whether he shot it and then it attacked, I don't know. In any event, the bear was able to get to him before it died. They both perished there, next to each other."

Stella looked up, her tears drying. "How can we

be absolutely sure it is Wesley? Did you find anything else?"

"I found the Winchester next to them. I brought it back. It's in the shed, along with the bear skull and Wesley's remains."

"I want to see him," said Stella firmly.

"Stella, you don't. There was no body after all these years."

"Well what did you bring back then? I want to know."

Thomas hesitated. "Are you sure?"

"Yes."

"All that remained was his skull," said Thomas, struggling to get the words out.

Stella gasped and looked down at the floor. Everyone was silent for what seemed like an eternity. Finally she stood.

"Thank you Thomas. Thank you for finding him and bringing him back," she said, hugging him tightly for a moment.

"I'm sorry," said Thomas.

"Don't be. I knew he was gone. The worst part was not knowing what happened to him. Now that I know, I can put him to rest."

With that, Stella put on a brave face and returned to normal, or at least it appeared that way to those that didn't know her well. Thomas could tell she was hurting inside, but was holding it in for Emily's benefit, not wanting to add to her sorrow. Thomas marveled at her resilience; she was a strong woman. Her attention now turned again to Emily and John.

"Emily, I know this is hard, but I will do anything I can to help you get through it," said Stella.

"Thank you Stella," she said, patting her reddened

eyes with her handkerchief. "Father, what are we to do now?"

"I don't know Emily. I don't think we should make any decisions today," said John.

"I think that's wise," said Stella.

* * *

The remainder of the day was somber. Thomas set about taking care of the bear hide while Stella tried to keep Emily busy. In the afternoon, John and Thomas took the hide and the sheep meat to town to sell.

John was hesitant about leaving Emily, but Stella assured him she would be fine. He was thankful Stella was there for his daughter. Even in the face of her own tragedy, her compassion flowed to others. *She is a remarkable woman*, thought John.

They returned from town late in the day to find Stella and Emily chatting on the porch, basking in the afternoon sun.

"I have dinner nearly ready," said Stella as they pulled up.

"How are you two doing?" asked Thomas.

"I'm going to be okay," said Emily. "It just all seems so unreal and distant."

"I know," said John, knowing the grief they shared would linger like an open wound for a long time.

"Put the horse away and come to dinner," said Stella as she headed for the kitchen.

Thomas took care of the wagon and horse while John escorted Emily to the dining room. Stella had already set the table and was busy carrying things from the kitchen.

"Let me help you," said Emily as she followed after her.

Once dinner was on and all were seated, Stella made an announcement.

"Tomorrow I would like to have a small ceremony to remember our loved ones."

"That would be nice," said Emily, her voice quivering as she struggled to fight back the tears.

"Thomas, I want to bury Wesley facing south, where the sun will always shine on him."

"I will ready things after dinner," said Thomas solemnly.

"I'll give you a hand," said John.

"Should we invite others to come and pay respects?" asked Thomas.

"No, I would like a private ceremony; just the four of us," said Stella. "Now, let's cheer up as best we can and enjoy our meal."

* * *

After dinner Thomas and John went to the shed to prepare for the next day. With limited materials to work with on short notice, Thomas fetched a wooden box that once held canned goods from the shelf, and lined it with the oil blanket he had purchased from Noel. There he placed Wesley's remains and folded the blanket over, carefully tucking it all around.

"John, please see if you can find some planks or slats for the top of the box. While you're doing that, I'll find a site and start digging," said Thomas as he grabbed a shovel from the corner of the shed and headed to the door.

"Will do," said John.

The ground behind the boarding house was south-facing and sloped gently upward. Thomas had the choice between it and a site towards the canyon entrance that was the same elevation as the house. For a moment he thought about asking Stella which she preferred but thought better of it. He would place the grave behind the boarding house, high enough up the slope so it could be seen by all travelers heading to and from the gold fields.

Thomas began to dig, but was soon through the shallow topsoil and into the jumble of big rocks, clay, and gravel that made up the glacial soils. As he headed back to the shed for a pick, he heard the sound of a hammer tapping away.

"How is it going?" asked Thomas as he entered the shed.

"Fine," said John. "I went ahead and nailed the top on the box."

Thomas took a look at it and nodded his approval.

"The ground is hard digging. I'll need this pickaxe to get down far enough."

"I'll come help you," said John.

They headed the short distance up the hill and worked together silently, swinging the pick and shoveling until they had a grave deep enough for the small box.

"We need a cross," said Thomas. "I want it to be big enough to be seen from the trail."

"We don't have any lumber," said John. "At least I didn't see any around the shed."

"We'll find a couple of small, straight spruce trees and skin the bark," said Thomas as he went to fetch an axe from the shed.

John and Thomas only had to walk a couple hundred yards to a small stand of spruce in order to find what they needed. They cut two trees, each about four inches in diameter, limbed them, and dragged both back to the shed. Thomas used a small saw to trim up the ends and cut the trees to length. It took a bit of digging around in the shed, but they found a drawknife and John set about removing the bark. With the bark removed, Thomas notched both logs and put them together forming the cross.

"Looks good," said John.

"Good, let's nail it," said Thomas.

John held the cross in place while Thomas spiked it together with four long nails.

"Now all we have to do is set it in place," said Thomas.

Together they carried the cross up the hill. Thomas labored with the shovel to dig a hole deep enough to set the cross in the ground. Fortunately he encountered no big rocks and they soon had the cross placed above the grave.

"I think we're ready for tomorrow," said Thomas.

"That was the easy part," John said solemnly as they gathered up the tools and headed back to the house.

Chapter 29

Morning dawned overcast and cool, typical of many days in the Alaskan summer. The weather seemed determined to dampen the spirits of those already afflicted.

At breakfast everyone was subdued. Emily finally broke the silence.

"Have you decided what we are going to do Father? Are we going home? I know Thomas wants to stay."

"Emily, everything we had is gone. I don't see any reason to rush back. Preston has taken care of everything that needs done."

"But what about money? Do we have enough to live on?"

"We still have our investments. Preston can wire us money anytime we need it. I checked with the telegraph office and it should be no problem," said John. "If Stella will have us, I'd like to stay on a while, maybe help out around here with some of the work needing done."

"You are welcome to stay as long as you like," said Stella.

"What about you Thomas?" asked John. "What are your immediate plans?"

Thomas thought for a moment and then smiled. "Keep on working towards a grubstake," he said.

"Emily, what do you want to do? Are you fine with staying here for at least part of the summer?" asked John.

Emily didn't hesitate. "Yes, as long as Thomas stays around."

"Then it's settled. Looks like you will have some guests for the summer Stella," said John.

"Sounds good," she said, smiling.

"When do you want to have the memorial service?"

asked Thomas, bringing their thoughts back to the present. "I think noon would be a good time," said Stella. "I have a couple of things to prepare."

* * *

By noon they had gathered in the dining room, each aware of the task before them.

"Thomas, please take this blanket to wrap the box," said Stella. "I crocheted this for Wesley shortly after we were married and I want him to be buried with it."

He took the folded blanket gently from her hands. "I'll meet all of you on the front porch in a moment. We can go up the hill together," said Thomas as he headed to the shed.

As he carefully wrapped the crude box housing Wesley's remains, Thomas admired Stella's handiwork. It was a beautiful blanket, made even more so by the love that went in to making it. Unknown to the others, the night before he had found a length of leather from an old harness and attached it to what was left of the Winchester rifle. Gathering up the box and the rifle, he headed to the front porch.

"Ready?" Thomas asked as he stepped up on the porch.

"Yes," said Stella as John and Emily nodded in agreement.

In silence they began the short procession up the gentle slope to the cross. Stella carried a wreath of wild flowers she made the night before, while Emily carried a single stem of wild rose. Thomas noticed John carried a well weathered book under his arm.

Thomas stopped, handed the rifle to John, then looked at Stella as he held the wrapped box in both hands. She paused for a long moment, staring out across the valley.

"Go ahead," said Stella quietly, her voice barely audible.

Emily was already crying softly. John moved closer and placed his free arm around her in an attempt to provide what little comfort he could.

Thomas knelt down by the grave and slowly lowered the box into it. He stood and looked at the others, wondering if he should speak. Just as the lingering silence became almost unbearable, John stepped forward.

"I would like to read something if I may," said John, handing the rifle back to Thomas and taking the book from under his arm.

"Please, go ahead," said Stella.

John opened the Bible, turned to a passage in Thessalonians, and read:

But I would not have you to be ignorant, brethren, concerning them which are asleep, that ye sorrow not, even as others which have no hope.

For if we believe that Jesus died and rose again, even so them also which sleep in Jesus will God bring with him.

For this we say unto you by the word of the Lord, that we which are alive and remain unto the coming of the Lord shall not prevent them which are asleep.

For the Lord himself shall descend from heaven with a shout, with the voice of the archangel, and with the trump of God: and the dead in Christ shall rise first:

Then we which are alive and remain shall be caught up together with them in the clouds, to meet the Lord in the air: and so shall we ever be with the Lord.

Wherefore comfort one another with these words.

John closed the book and looked up. With his voice breaking, he said "May God rest the souls of our lost loved ones."

Emily was crying openly now and Stella had tears slowly making their way down her face. Thomas stood firm, trying to keep it together.

"Thank you for those words, John. They were very comforting," said Stella, wiping tears from her cheek. "Wesley used to always read to me from the Bible."

Though Thomas didn't quite fathom what John had read, he was happy it brought some comfort to Stella.

"It's time," said Stella. She stepped forward and scooped up a small handful of dirt. "Wesley, we followed our dreams to this land. I am alone now. I can only imagine what might have been." She paused, looking down. "Goodbye Wesley; I will forever love you," she said as she slowly released the contents of her hand into the grave.

Through her tears, Emily took the rose and dropped it into the grave. "Goodbye Mother. I will miss you dearly," she said before breaking down and sobbing loudly.

"Thomas, would you care to say something?" asked Stella, her voice quivering ever so slightly.

He knew this was coming. He didn't deal with death well, yet he knew he was expected to say something. "Yes," he said, staring at the ground. Silence covered the hillside for what seemed like a long time, each waiting to hear what Thomas would say.

Finally he spoke. "Lydia, your husband loves you,

your daughter cherishes you, it was a pleasure to know you. You will be greatly missed."

Thomas paused for a moment, gathering his thoughts. Stella was standing close, looking up at him to see what he would say next.

"Wesley, I never knew you, but feel like I do. You were a hard working man, a good provider and husband to Stella. She has missed you all these years and now, finally, you are home. I wish I had been able to call you my friend."

"Thank you Thomas," said Stella, hugging him firmly. She paused, then said, "I want to place this wreath on the grave."

Thomas took this as a signal to complete the burial. He and John worked quickly yet reverently to close the grave. When they were done, Stella knelt and laid the wreath, placed two fingers to her lips, then touched the small cross hidden amongst the flowers and leaves of the wreath. As she stood, she turned and hugged Emily, then extended her hands to her and John. Thomas took the rifle and hung it from the cross, then took Emily's free hand.

"It is done," said Stella.

As they walked slowly down the hill, hand in hand, tears still flowing, the sun broke radiantly through the clouds. Tomorrow would be bright; a new beginning.

* * *

About the Author

G.E. Sherman has a wide and varied background, including that of geologist, mining engineer, software engineer, and author. He has authored both technical books and articles, as well as fiction. In addition to being the founder of the popular open source QGIS project, he has published a number of books on the topic.

When writing fiction, he draws on the depth of his background, providing vivid descriptions of life on the last frontier, wildlife encounters, and survival. Further, his experience as an outdoor enthusiast provides inspiration in the stories he tells.

G.E. Sherman resides in Alaska and regularly watches moose from his living room window.

Made in the USA
Monee, IL
14 March 2021